SQUIRREL APOCALYPSE

SQUIRREL APOCALYPSE

JOSEF MATULICH

Hydra
Publications

ISBN: 978-1-948374-23-1

Hydra Publications

Goshen, Kentucky 40026

www.hydrapublications.com

To my Literary Wingman Sheldon Gleisser, who has been with me through every stage of this project, from the time Timur Bekmambetov spoiled it for me as a screenplay, through the novel pitch sessions and edits. This is all your fault.

FLYING SQUIRREL

(Northern California, 1990)

The western gray squirrel approached Chris's invention in slow, nervous steps. It followed its nose, just like that stupid toucan from the cereal commercials, drawn in by the scent of peanut butter. It was a potent lure. The rodent set one foot on the metal base of the COR Squirrel Launcher Mk VII, which was bolted into a tree stump at the edge of the woods.

The squirrel sniffed.

To get at the food, it would have to climb onto the spring-loaded mechanism and out to the end of the swinging arm. The squirrel took some time to convince itself the reward was worth the risk.

The squirrel began to climb.

Chris crouched out of their target's line of sight and held onto the trip wire. He clamped his other hand over his mouth and nose to keep from exploding into giggles. Olivia, on the other side of the blind, was having just as much trouble keeping quiet. Rafael, he was almost always silent. He stared through the viewfinder of Grandma's video camera with the grim determination of a sniper with a high-power rifle. Chris held up one finger on his trigger hand, asking them to hang on, and they nodded back.

The squirrel franticly flicked its tail as it crept down the moment arm and licked away at the mound of peanut butter. Chris waited until he was sure that the animal was completely focused on the free meal and then pulled as hard as he could on the wire. The arm of the modified skeet launcher swung around, like a headsman's ax. It pitched the rodent into the air, like a clay pigeon. It flew, gyrating on all axes as it did, up between two trees selected by the kids as their goalposts. The flying squirrel chittered and squealed as it disappeared into the leafy branches.

Chris almost felt bad for that, but Grandma had taught him that squirrels are not really like all of God's other creatures. They are sly, avaricious, and pure evil. Her opinion of them was tainted by the fact that a squirrel had killed Grandpa forty-some years ago.

He was out hunting and needed to climb over a barbed wire fence. While he was poised, in the most delicate way, over the top wire, a ground squirrel climbed Grandpa's shotgun, which was leaned up against the fence. When its pink little toes settled on the trigger, it pumped two rounds of buckshot into Grandpa's spleen and testicles.

Grandma, to this day, said it was premeditated. That crime outweighed all the torments the three kids had heaped upon that squirrel's distant relatives over the last summer.

Chris whooped in victory, jumping up and down with his fists over his head, as did Olivia. Rafael just kept shooting to document this stunt for history, or at least for Grandma. She never grew tired of seeing squirrels suffer.

"That was perfect!" Olivia shouted. Then she rushed over and threw her arms around Chris's neck. Caught up in the excitement, she kissed him on the cheek.

Chris stopped jumping up and down. Never having been kissed by a girl, he was stunned. He looked over to Rafael to see what his friend's reaction would be, but all he saw was the camera lens and the fold out display.

Olivia made that little face which usually meant *Boys are such idiots* and went over to Rafael. Pulling the camera down away from his face, she gave him a kiss on the cheek, too.

"Are we good?" she asked.

Before either one could answer, a high-pitched screech carried through the trees.

"Christopher, you mom's here!"

"Oh, crap, time to go," Chris muttered.

"You're going back home now?" Rafael folded the camera shut and clicked the lens cap into place before sticking it in its carrying bag.

"Got to," Chris said. "I start seventh grade in two days."

Olivia kicked her toe in the leaf litter near the stump. Her white tennies were covered with hand-painted yellow and pink flowers, just like the ones on the clip in her blonde hair. Sometimes, when they were terrorizing the local populace, he forgot how pretty she was.

"Well, we're going to miss you," she said.

Rafael swung the carrying case by its strap while saying nothing.

"Yeah." Rafael finally spoke. He looked the way he always

did, like he was working very hard to look like nothing at all. "You'll be back next summer, right?"

"Chris!" Grandma screeched again. "Where are you hiding, you little rodent?"

All three kids flinched.

Olivia wrapped Chris up in a quick hug and then released him.

He turned to Rafael, with his hand extended for a shake.

Rafael brought up his hand, which closed into a fist, and he punched Chris in the shoulder, just hard enough for them both to know it.

"I'll be bigger next year," Chris couldn't say why, but it was important to him that, one day, he'd earn Rafael's respect for his muscle, instead of just his brains.

"You think so, *pendejo?*" Rafael's smile came easy, much more easy than words.

Chris was about to make a brilliant response, but he was interrupted.

"And where the hell is my Goddamn video camera?" Grandma shouted in the distance.

Chris bolted at the sound, running down the path to Grandma's house, before he even knew what he was doing.

Rafael sprinted after, passing off the camera case, like a baton in a relay.

Chris waved over his shoulder as he went. "See you two next year!"

* * *

The agouti-gray squirrel tumbled through the air, struck a tree nine feet up from the ground, and then bounced sideways. It made its descent down the wooded hill like a steel ball in a

Pachinko machine, bouncing from trunk to trunk. It emitted little chirps and squeals with each impact, playing a fast-paced, anguished song. The flight ended in the gravel bank above a stream, where the rodent slid to a stop with its rump and tail in the water.

The battered beast let out a wheezing gasp, as if saying to itself, "*Oy, Gevelt.*"

The Sciuriologist had been doing an ecological survey scant yards away when the rodent had fallen down the hill. Making long swishing strides in hip-waders, she came up to the squirrel and scooped it up in her black rubber gloves.

"Don't worry, my love," she cooed. "you, and your descendants of a hundred generations, will have your revenge."

DEATH AND PORK BELLIES

(Twenty years later)

Everything Chris Day had left of his life was strapped to the top of his old Land Rover, or stuffed in the back. That included his tween-age daughter, Liv, who laid across the back seat, languishing. She refused to wear her seat belt. Two hundred miles ago, she had declared that being catapulted out of a crashing car sounded like way more fun than a stay at Great-Grandma's house.

The Black-Eyed Peas sputtered out on the radio, right between "Boom Boom" and "Pow," to leave behind only background static. Chris hit the tuner buttons, from left from to right, with nothing but white noise and ghost voices coming out of the speakers.

"Oh, great," Liv groaned, "we're so far from civilization that radio waves can't reach us."

"Hang on a second." He shifted over to the AM band and started at the bottom of the spectrum. "Baby, you know this only temporary. Just until we get back on our feet."

"Unless we get eaten by wild animals first."

As he cranked the tuner, he heard a parade of twanging country chords, angry talk, and invocations of Jesus. Things were sounding bleak. He and his daughter might have to actually speak to each other for the last leg of the trip.

"Some of the best days of my life were here." He was about to tell her some of the old stories, like about the time when they built a temporary corral around the Cunninghams' prize bull while he slept in the pasture, but she beat him to the punch.

"You and Olivia and Rafael... the three musketeers... pranks and hijinks... friends for life."

Chris grimaced as he flicked through a station that was playing a bluegrass version of "Brain Damage."

"And I thought you never listened to me."

If Liv had another snarky response, Chris never heard it. A woman's voice, smooth and sleek as buttered sex on toast, read the news over the top end of the AM band.

"...And feed lot hogs sold for three-ninety-five on the Chicago Mercantile Exchange."

It took Chris a few moments to comprehend what she was saying. It didn't matter, as long as she said it in that voice.

"Well, hello, beautiful. Tell me more." Parts of his anatomy which had shriveled up since the divorce came alive at the sound.

"Dad, she's talking about pigs."

Chris sighed dreamily. "She could be talking about flesh-eating bacteria, and I'd listen, all day long, to that voice."

His daughter summoned up a non-vocal expression of disgust, as only a twelve-year-old girl could.

The Voice continued on the radio. "It's twelve o'clock, Wednesday noon, and KILT now honors the recently departed of Humboldt County."

Liv raised her head up from the backseat to look at Chris in disgust.

"What?"

"Harold Phillip Grimes," the Voice purred, "aged fifty-six, was killed in an accident in the marshmallow plant..."

Chris drummed his thumbs on the steering wheel.

"Yup, that's what's she's reading."

"And you still want to listen to that?"

Chris glanced in the mirror to see the expression on Liv's face, one that children have been using to display dismay and disgust for their parents since the days when humans and Neanderthals stopped interbreeding.

"For a little while..."

* * *

The Voice had finished with the dead folk of Humboldt County as Chris and Liv hit the last leg of their trip. Cruising along Highway 99 between pastures filled with grazing dairy cows, they passed the sign that read: *Crickson, CA, pop. 3500.* There were several more bullet holes in the sign than the last time he'd been here, and broken beer bottles formed a pile beneath it.

"Oh, great," Liv muttered. "How far until we get to the tractor-pull and cow-tipping stadium?"

Chris drove on without comment. The turn to Grandma's house was just a bit farther down on the left.

Finally, the Land Rover came to a stop in Grandma Day's driveway just outside her back porch. Her yard had gotten even denser during the last two decades, occupied with an army of brightly-colored metal sculptures, whirligigs, and squirrel-proof bird feeders. A dozen different wind chimes tinkled with the light breeze.

Chris came out of the car slowly, his joints and muscles frozen from the eight hours behind the wheel.

Liv came out the driver's side behind him, her eyes wide, and her jaw slack. "Did Grandma's house always look like *this*?"

Chris chuckled. That was the way most people reacted at first.

"She has always been a little…"

"Deranged hoarder?"

"Eccentric," Chris corrected. "Though, she does have an obsession with—"

Chris saw the squirrel in the branches behind Liv's head at the same time that he heard the back porch door being thrown open behind him. The sound of a pump shotgun jacking a shell into the chamber came just a second later. Liv was looking the other way when he tackled her and threw her to the ground behind the car.

"SQUIRREL!" Grandma screamed as she loosed two rounds in their direction.

The shots tore two holes in the branches above them; leaves fluttered down around Liv and Chris's heads. The rodent must have been untouched, since it leaped away through the branches, chattering bloody murder.

Looking back toward the house under his car, Chris saw a pair of fluffy bunny slippers clump down the stairs and across the driveway.

"You're damn right, you fluffy little tree-rat!" Grandma shouted. "Come back here, and I'll nail your furry little ass!"

She had come around the Rover far enough to see father and daughter cowering on the tarmac.

"Chris, what are you doing down there?" the scrawny old lady in the flowered housedress asked.

"Good to see you, Grandma," Chris said as calmly as possible under the circumstances.

"Is she going to shoot us?" Liv teetered on the edge of shock.

"It's only rock salt here around the house. Gentler than they deserve." Grandma laid her twelve-gauge shotgun on the Rover's hood. "If squirrels ate meat, it would be the end of Western civilization."

She leaned down and took Liv's hand to pull her to her feet with practically no effort.

Chris stood and dusted off his clothes.

"C'mere and give your great-grandmother a hug." The old lady wrapped up the girl in bare, speckled arms and began to squeeze.

Liv looked her dad's way with a silent plea for help displayed on her face.

Chris picked up the shotgun, locked in the safety, and headed for the porch. "Liv," Chris said, "why don't you get the bags?

Grandma released her, and Liv sprang to retrieving their bags from the back of the Land Rover. She was amazingly eager to be helpful when gunplay might be involved.

Grandma sidled up to Chris, a misty smile on her face.

"Little one's growing up fast. Looks just like her mother."

"Uh-hmm."

"Any word from the bitch?"

"She seems singularly disinterested in communicating." He hated to admit how bad things had gotten, but pride wasn't something he had excesses of lately. "I forged Liv's last two birthday cards from Amber."

Grandma made a quiet, pained noise. "You think Liv knows?"

"I caught her practicing her mom's signature, and doing it better than me."

Grandma pulled him down into a hug, a little awkward now that he was eight inches taller than her. "You're welcome here for as long as you want."

"Thanks, Grandma."

She let him go and patted his cheek. "Since you have an engineering degree from that fancy school out east, I'm sure you could fix a few things at the dairy to earn your keep."

SQUIRREL IN A BLENDER

The Judas Squirrel was sent out of the hedgerow to stand alone in the clearing, looking harmless and delicious. A Cooper's hawk circled high over the pasture, looking for something edible that wouldn't put up too much of a fight.

The rodent purposely turned its back to the predator and began to groom itself. It presented an irresistible target that took only a few minutes for the hawk to spot. As the bird dropped toward its intended meal, the Sentinel Squirrels in adjacent trees chirped out range, speed, and direction to warn the Judas. It kept still, with its back exposed until the final moment.

The hawk descended toward the squirrel, with talons extended and wings spread to envelop its prey, only to find that lunch had run out before the raptor hit the ground. It pulled itself together, tucked in its wings, and scanned the area with its sharp beak open, as if it were gasping to itself and muttering, "What the fuck?"

Naturally, the hawk wasn't that confused. The squirrel ran

away. That's what squirrels do. The bird was simply processing details to come up with the most efficient Plan B to put calories in its stomach without expending too many during the catching.

The Judas squirrel flicked its tail a few times, a flag to keep the interest of a predator. After several glances out of either side of its head, the hawk swooped into the dark space beneath the bushes, still thinking that it was the predator.

The Avenger Squirrels struck first. They had the markings and temperament of Rottweilers, though they still were squirrels. The Avengers weighed in at three times the mass of a Cooper's hawk. When they laid into it, the bird had only enough time for one high-pitched keen. Once the bird was down and pinioned, the other squirrels joined in the ambush. The sound was closer to a wolf pack savaging an elk than the clicks and chirps of hungry rodents. Feathers, blood, and dark meat were thrown in every direction.

The Judas Squirrel came back out with its own portion of the kill. It gnawed the meat off of one yellow talon and then cleaned the blood off of its fur. With luck, there would be another starving predator in the pasture before dark.

* * *

Chris walked down the main drag of Crickson, immersed in a sense of nostalgia.

Liv trudged along behind and carried the groceries.

Chris pointed out the highpoints of the local color. "The diner and the tractor supply are down that road."

"Thrilling."

"But, just past that is Crickson Funland, miniature golf and soft-serve ice cream."

"That's what you did during the days before TV?"

A woman's voice chimed in from behind them, "When we weren't painting pictures of mastodons on cave walls."

Chris turned to see a woman, probably around his age, blonde and very pretty, in a soccer mom blazer and mom jeans kind of way. The two boys with her, one blonde like her, and one Latino, added to the suburban parent vibe. She smiled as if she knew him.

"Kids have no sense of history," she said, "do they?"

The dots finally came together inside Chris's mind. There were no flowered tennies, or barrettes, but he'd recognize this girl anywhere.

"Olivia?"

"Your grandmother told me you were coming back for a visit," she said.

Liv set down the groceries and groaned, "With no time off for good behavior."

Olivia chuckled at the remark. The boys' expressions, shielded from Olivia, were more like sympathy.

"She did mention you were in town," Chris said.

"Just mentioned?" Olivia raised an eyebrow. "I thought she would try harder than that. If you and I were dating, she could expect free radio advertising for the dairy."

It took Chris a moment to parse out exactly what she'd said. "You work at KILT?" he asked.

"I own it," she said, but then shrugged, "Well, me and the bank and assorted creditors."

"That must have taken a lot of maneuvering."

"Well, I had help back then."

All three kids grew restive at the boring adult talk.

Olivia ruffled the blonde boy's hair.

"I know," she teased, "the Xbox is calling your name. We'll get going in just a second."

Chris pointed at the matched set of boys. He noticed that the blonde was wearing an anime T-shirt, while the brown-haired boy sported Neil DeGrasse Tyson.

"So who are these guys?"

"This is my son, Dakota," Olivia laid her hand on the shoulder of the blonde, freckled one. "And his best friend, Cesar."

She smiled at Liv, then said, "It looks like you all will be going to class together next week."

"Instant friends," Liv muttered. "Terrific."

The boys waved at their new classmate.

"Hi," said Dakota.

"Yeah, hi," said Cesar.

"Whatever." Liv picked up the grocery-filled bags as a sign she wanted to go, too.

A green pick-up from the '70s drove by, its horn honking as a gray-haired Asian lady waved. Chris saw its tailgate was covered with stickers for KILT, NORML, and a black on yellow bumper sticker declaring: *SQUIRREL IN A BLENDER.*

"Gee, you know everybody here," Chris said with a chuckle.

"Well, yeah, but *she* works at the station."

Her explanation got cut off by the whoop of a police siren. A sheriff's green and white SUV pulled up alongside them, and the passenger's side window rolled down. A Latino man in uniform fumed behind the wheel. He, too, looked familiar to Chris.

"Cesar!" the man snapped. "Aren't you supposed to be home right now?"

Cesar flinched at the sound of his name.

Olivia and Dakota both bowed their heads, as if they'd just been caught shoplifting.

"Morning, Rafael," Olivia said quietly.

"Miss Halverson." Rafael acknowledged her and dismissed

her in the same four syllables. He shifted his focus back onto Cesar. "Get in the truck."

"Tio Rafael," Cesar whined.

"Don't 'Uncle' me. You have a stack of summer reading on the dining room table you haven't finished. Get in the truck, now."

Cesar sullenly slumped his way to the truck and climbed inside.

Rafael began dressing him down, his words low and quick. "Cesar Alejandro Carnicero, how many times have I told you not to hang around with those trash? You think people aren't watching everything we do?" The tirade continued as the SUV drove away.

"He did not look happy to see you," Chris said. "He didn't even recognize me."

Olivia exhaled and rolled her eyes. "Don't worry, he knew it was you."

"Really?"

"It's complicated," Olivia said. "Look, I've got to go. I'll be seeing you later. It's a really small town."

She put a hand in the middle of Dakota's back and guided him off the other way.

Chris watched them disappear for a minute or two. Then, he took the grocery bags from Liv and walked back to the car. Blessedly, Liv was silent, too.

She waited until they were back in the Rover before she said anything. "Yeah, the fun times are really gonna roll now that the Three Musketeers are back together."

HEMP & ELBOW GREASE

J ohn and Mandy Cunningham leaped out of either side of their rusty, old pickup, as quickly as they could, once it came to a stop. Since they were sixty-six and sixty-two, respectively, it wasn't all that fast. The woman announcer on the radio spurred them on to their best, though.

"As a service to the horticultural segment of Humboldt County," she reported in a smoldering, sexy voice, "KILT continues our coverage of the movements of the sheriff's patrol and the DEA."

John went up to his lean-to just inside the tree-line around their cultivated field. He threw off a green tarp to reveal several bundles of dried cannabis plants bound in canvas and twine. He picked up the top bundle, which was nearly as tall and wide as he was. John staggered toward the bed of the truck, bumping into obstacles all along the way.

Mandy dropped the tailgate for him and guided him in the last few inches.

"Three SUVs belonging to the Sheriff and DEA are heading

north on Route Thirty-five, north of Hempstead," the sultry voice on the radio continued.

"They're headed our way!" Mandy shouted.

"I know! I know!" He pitched his bundle into the truck and went back for another.

The two of them stacked pot plants into the bed until they were piled up to the roof.

"National Guard helicopters are also making sweeps across the western half of the county."

As John threw ropes over the load to secure it, Mandy ducked into the back of the lean-to for their fifteen-pound bag of seed. As she came out, she heard something skittering on the roof. When she turned to check what it was, she saw a black and tan animal that looked like a cross between a Doberman and wolverine.

It snarled at her as they locked eyes.

Mandy shrieked as she dropped sack of seed and ran. "John! Start the truck now, John!" Mandy bounced into the passenger seat, like a jackrabbit, and locked the door behind her.

"You get the seeds?" John asked.

"The mountain lion's eating them."

John wheeled around in his seat to get a look at the lean-to. Just in front of it, the strange black and tan animal was tearing open the sack and gobbling up the seeds.

"That's not a mountain lion, I don't think"

"I don't care what it is," Mandy snapped. "Just drive!"

"You got it!"

As John shifted the truck into first and hit the gas, the announcer concluded her program on the radio, "We at KILT hope this information will be of service to the agricultural entrepreneurs of our county. And, remember, the cops will get theirs one day, because karma is like—"

Martha looked into the outrigger mirror and saw as many as a dozen squirrels joining the big black and tan thing to chow down on the marijuana seeds.

John switched off the radio in disgust. "Yeah, thanks, KILT."

Mandy watched the gathering herd of squirrels disappear in the distance. As she felt her heart pound in her chest, she wondered what a stoned squirrel might do. That, and what the hell that Doberman/weasel thing was.

Both husband and wife calmed down a bit as they drove through the federal lands to the back route to their home.

John even patted her knee and chuckled. "The things we do to pay the bills," he said.

His good mood evaporated pretty damn quickly as soon as they came around the bend and saw the roadblock ahead. He knocked it into neutral and stomped the brakes.

Mandy gripped the Jesus bar and braced against the dashboard. The truck lurched and nosed down under its load.

Just as they realized the trucks and Hummers across the road were not police, or DEA, the load came loose, and bundles of marijuana fell off to either side of the bed.

"Oh, great," they both said at the same time.

Abraham Vizcarra, and perhaps a dozen of his business associates, stood waiting in front of the vehicles. Except for the man with the hundred-dollar haircut, they were all dirty, sullen warriors covered in greens and browns, the kind of men you see on the cable news when there's war, or less organized violence, anywhere in the world.

Mandy had no idea what kind of assault rifles the men carried but, from the look on their faces, she was pretty sure that they enjoyed using them.

Mandy clutched John's hand and squeezed for all she was worth.

He nodded reassurance to her, but with the smallest, slowest movement possible to avoid provoking the armed men.

Vizcarra strolled up to John's side of the truck, looking cool in his white linen suit and open-necked shirt. He signaled for them to roll down the window as his gunmen shouldered their weapons and aimed through the windshield.

"What a pleasant surprise to see you out here, Mrs. Cunningham. Mr. Cunningham." He smiled like a social director on a cruise ship. "Have you had a chance to consider our business proposal?"

* * *

Chris hung, head first, into the guts of the dairy's refrigeration compressor. Only his belt buckle caught on the lip of the casing kept him from falling in. As he hung there, suspended between Earth and a broken nose, he tightened the fittings on the ammonia coolant pipes. He finished the job with a grunt and a 'simplesunuvabitch'.

He extricated himself from the machinery, something that was much more difficult than falling in when gravity did its part. He threw the wrench to the floor, with a clatter, and hit the power switch.

The machinery began to move, painfully slow and groaning, like Grandma getting to kitchen for her morning coffee. Chris checked the pressure and flow gauges. Every needle stayed within the green optimal ranges.

Chris gave himself a "thumbs up" and a grunt of victory.

A faint squeal came from the heart of the machinery.

It built in intensity, a steady, intermittent squeak. It sounded like a hamster lost its footing on an exercise wheel and then let out a yelp of pain each time the wheel dropped it on its head.

That's a bearing in the pump system. Chris sighed. He could only access it, through an entirely different hatch, with a whole different set of tools. *Maybe I can pull it and repack it before dinner,* he thought.

* * *

Five hours later, he left the dairy building and blinked at the fading sunlight. He clenched and unclenched his hands, trying to get them out of the tool-handle shaped claws they'd become. He clumsily opened the Land Rover and slid inside. He checked his face in the rearview mirror. He was covered in grease and dirt. His hair stood up in multiple directions, due to God knew what kind of crap that was in it.

If he saw someone who looked like him on the street, he would have guessed that the guy had been in some kind of explosion.

He sat behind the wheel, not having the energy to shut the door, or start the engine.

"Well," he said. "That should be good for my room and board. For the next five years."

Eventually, he got his ass in gear, and the car with it, and headed for home. He was serenaded on the radio with the sexy voice of KILT reporting the movements of the DEA.

GONE TO POT

C hris saw a bedraggled old couple walking alongside the road. He squinted at them and looked very carefully. He wasn't completely sure he wasn't hallucinating them out of exhaustion. When they didn't flicker like a mirage, he chuckled to himself and pulled over in front of them.

As the dust settled, and they climbed in, Chris was pleased to see that they were who he thought they were: the Cunningham's, the owners of the dairy farm adjacent to his grandmother's property.

The look on Mrs. Cunningham's face was a combination of astonishment and concern when she saw Chris, "Dear Lord, Son, did you get yourself blown up?"

"No, just worked inside some of the machinery at the dairy." Chris patted down his wild hair as best as he could.

She relaxed at hearing his explanation. Sagged, really.

"Thank you so very much for stopping for us," Mrs. Cunningham said. She looked like he felt, somewhere past the edge of collapse.

"Anything for you two," Chris replied. The smiling old lady in the front seat of the Rover felt like more of a grandmother to Chris than Grandma Day did. He had probably eaten a thousand cookies at her kitchen table and washed it down with ten gallons of raw milk while Grandma was away on dairy business.

"Yeah," Mr. Cunningham said from the back seat, "I thought we were going to be walking all the way home."

"Well, I'm glad I came along at the right time," Chris said. "Remember how we used to have milk fights in the dairy barn? I'm glad the cows didn't mind my squeezing their udders like that."

"We don't have the cows anymore, Chris," Mr. Cunningham said. "Couldn't make a go of it."

"You're kidding," Chris exclaimed. "That's a shame. You loved those cows."

"Love doesn't pay the bills," Mr. Cunningham sighed. "And the love of a cow is illegal in most states."

Chris laughed, probably too loudly because of exhaustion.

Mrs. Cunningham leaned back to slap her husband's knee to discipline him, but she couldn't reach. She swung at him a few more times, anyway.

The song on the radio ended, and the Voice cut in for station identification. Half of Chris's brain fixated on her as the Cunninghams spoke.

A Humboldt County Sheriff's green and white SUV came up the other direction on the narrow road. Chris smiled and waved as it passed. His passengers sat bolt upright and fell silent.

"So what are you doing nowadays?"

"Oh, you know," Mrs. Cunningham said, "a little this, a little that."

"A little more that than the other," Mr. Cunningham added. He was twisted around to look at the sheriff's truck going the other way. It made a wide U-turn and started after them with its blue and red lights flashing.

"Remember, folks, karma is like a squirrel in a blender," the Voice declared.

Mrs. Cunningham switched off the radio before the Voice could complete her thought.

"I wonder what the hell he wants," Chris muttered, more to himself than as an actual question.

"Well, how on Earth would we know?" Mrs. Cunningham said sweetly.

Chris pulled over to the side and waited for the cop to tell them what he wanted. He made sure to keep his hands high up on the steering wheel, easily visible. His fingers tapped on the wheel as he watched the rearview mirror and waited for the officer to come out.

After enough time to read off his license plates and collect his driving records and permanent high school record, the driver's door opened, and the officer stepped out. It was Rafael, again.

"Crap!" Chris spat out.

"I know why I'm saying 'Crap,' " Mr. Cunningham said, "but why on Earth are you saying 'Crap'?"

Chris examined plain and folksy old Mr. Cunningham that he knew from childhood and realized that he really had no idea who this man was.

"Is there something you want to tell me?"

Mr. Cunningham responded with a gallows grin, "It's too late for that now."

Rafael approached the Rover in a slow, angry swagger. Chris had the feeling that he was going to get pulled out the window and stomped with steel-toe boots. In spite of the premonition, Chris rolled down the window before Rafael had to ask.

"License and registration, please."

Chris only saw his own greasy reflection in Rafael's mirrored lenses. He nodded and leaned across the stick shift, and Mrs. Cunningham, to retrieve his papers from the glove box.

"Here you go," Chris said as he surrendered the papers. "Is everything okay, Rafael?"

"I would prefer it if you called me Corporal Carnicero when I'm on duty."

"Sorry, Corporal Carnicero, I meant no disrespect."

"I'll also answer to 'sir,' if you're in a hurry."

"Okay, sir."

Rafael looked over the documents as if they were forged in crayon. A sour grimace pulled his mouth to one side.

"Do you know why I stopped you?"

"Was I driving too slow?" Chris asked. "I'm really tired, I just spent the last twelve hours fixing machinery at the milk-processing plant, and I didn't want to be moving any faster than I could really handle..."

"Seat belts."

"You're kidding me." Chris swiveled his head around to check his passengers. Neither one had their shoulder harnesses on.

"It's a primary offense in this state." Cpl. Carnicero, sir, pulled out his ticket pad and a pen.

Mr. and Mrs. Cunningham remained silent. They looked like smiling mannequins in an AARP online clothing store.

"I guess they didn't have a chance to buckle up." Chris tried to slick down his hair so he didn't look so much like he was in an accident in a meth lab. He swore his hair crackled as he pushed it into place. "I just picked them up a minute ago."

"I see." The officer tapped his pen against his pad as he

looked over the twelve-year-old Rover. "Could you step out of the vehicle, please?"

"Okay."

Chris did his best not to look unsteady as he stepped out of the car, even though he felt dead on his feet. Standing next to him, Chris could see that his old friend had had a much bigger growth spurt in his teenage years than he had. Cpl. Carnicero, sir, was six inches taller than he was with the body of an athlete. He, no doubt, lifted weights while Chris pushed code and CAD/CAM for the last ten years.

Rafael could kick his ass without breathing hard, even without the gun on his hip, or the Taser, or the pepper spray, or the wooden police baton with the sideways handle.

The officer moved toward the back of the Rover in steady, measured steps.

Chris followed. "It looks like you've switched from mechanical squirrel launchers to explosives," Cpl. Carnicero remarked.

"I did not get blown up!"

The corporal nodded minutely. "So are these two friends of yours?"

"They're locals," Chris said. "Don't you know them?"

"The important question is: Do you know them?"

"Well, of course, I know them." Chris was moving away from terrified, to astounded, at his friend's combination of hostility and stupidity. "They used to babysit me when Grandma was away."

"They're sensimilla farmers now."

Chris had no idea what that was, but he had a guess. He went with that instead of admitting absolute ignorance.

"Those are like chinchillas, right?"

"It's pot." Cpl. Carnicero's expression soured, indicating that he thought even less of Chris now than when he did when they'd started this conversation. "Really carefully cultivated marijuana. They grow it on the federal land north of town.

"Oh."

Cpl. Carnicero craned his neck and inspected the vehicle from the outside, silently letting Chris and the Cunninghams stew for a minute or two.

"It would be an incredible coincidence," he finally said, "for me to find you in the company of known drug producers after I first saw you with their biggest enablers."

"Enablers?"

"Olivia Halverson at KILT thinks it's cute to warn pot farmers of our movements on the air."

Somehow, he didn't register that the sexy descriptions of DEA and police movements connected to anything in the real world. Chris grimaced at the thought of crazed drug dealers, waiting for the cops, with shotguns and AK47s. No wonder Rafael was so pissed.

"Nobody's gotten hurt, have they?" Chris asked.

"Not yet."

Rafael pounded his notebook against his hand as he looked out at the fields laid out for hay, or pasturage, beside the road.

"You might want to be more careful of the company you keep here in Crickson." He handed back Chris's papers. "We'll save the search and seizure for the next time."

He secured his pen and notebook almost absently. With the mirrored glasses still in place, Chris had difficulty reading his old friend.

"Have a nice day." Rafael went back and got into his vehicle.

Chris slid back behind the wheel of the Rover, pulling the door shut, quickly, to avoid having it torn off as Rafael sped away. As he spoke to Mr. and Mrs. Cunningham, he knew that he had the same tone and expression as when he had to talk to Liv about eighty dollars in overage charges on last month's phone bill.

"Marijuana? Really?"

Mr. Cunningham was cowed in the back seat. Mrs. Cunningham was more forthcoming in her response. "It's not as simple as all that. There's not enough money in milk to keep everybody in business, especially with the recession and a bunch of people losing their homes."

"Uh-huh." Chris tapped his fingers on the steering wheel, still in parent mode with this couple who had gone to school with his grandmother. "It's all pretty disappointing."

"Oh, come off it," Mr. Cunningham said. "You were twelve when you last stayed the summer here. Folks were doing what they had to to survive long before that."

"Yeah, right."

Chris put the Rover in gear and started off for the Cunningham place. He reminded himself to check under the seats for anything those two might have hidden while he spoke with Rafael.

CESAR'S SHOP OF HORRORS

L iv walked alone against the stream of students between classes, with her books clutched across her chest. She was headed to her locker to drop off her books and see what the Board of Education classified as food. Liv had only minimal interest in socializing with the cow and tractor crowd. They hadn't broken their legs to leap up and make her feel welcome, either. Her plan was to find something vaguely digestible and stake out a spot at the table reserved for newbies and lepers.

It was really the way she wanted it. With her luck, something would happen again, and she and Dad would end up someplace even less civilized than this. Somalia, probably.

"Psssst!"

That sound either meant someone was trying to get her attention, or she was about to be attacked by a really big snake. She was rooting for the snake. She kept walking, hoping her death would be quick.

"Psssst! Hey, Liv!"

Since she hadn't given her names to any snakes, this had to be one of the two dweebs her father wanted her to hang with. There he was, standing in the alcove that led into the restrooms, and waving like a Happy Cat on somebody's dashboard.

"Hi, Liv," Dakota whispered.

"Um, hi," she whispered back. She hated every single person in this new school, but she still didn't want them seeing her talking to *him*. "On the run from the law, are we?"

"Just being discrete." He pushed his messy blonde hair out of his face to have it fall right back down. It looked like shit, but at least it wasn't a mullet. "You have lunch next period, right?

The crowd was thinning out in the hall as the next bell came up. She took a step or two closer, but not close enough for him to grab her.

"Why you asking?"

"Cesar and I have a secret hideout."

Liv looked up at the restroom signs, at the same time putting her hand on the metal cylinder in her back pocket:

"I've got pepper spray."

"There's nothing to worry about. You can see Cesar's collection."

That sounded as much fun as a nine-hour road trip with her father, but trying to find a clique-free seat in the cafeteria, without drama, might possibly be worse.

"What does he collect?" Liv asked.

"Everything," Dakota said with more pride than his buddy probably deserved.

* * *

Dakota led her down a series of halls, the normal cinderblock middle school crap with inspirational bulletin boards and event posters for things like autumn festivals, or tractor pulls. Liv wondered how much trouble she would be in if these two tried something and she had to pepper spray them and then stomp them with her Doc Martens.

Dakota stopped at a heavy wooden door marked *Cleaning Supplies*, and he opened it for her.

She read the sign just below it, *Employees Only* and gave the boy a dubious look.

Dakota puffed up, like this might be something to be proud of, too, "I know people."

She gestured for him to go first, seeming polite to him, but a great way to ruin ambushes, too. She put down her books to keep the door from locking behind her and followed the dweeb into the supply closet.

* * *

The lights were low. Jars and bottles filled shelves on all the walls. Dead things in yellow fluid occupied most of the containers. Almost every available flat spot Liv could see held furs, bones, and odd artifacts. Cesar was working on more, cleaning what looked like a cow skull with a toothbrush. Since no one sprang out from behind the door with a rag and a bottle of chloroform, Liv came in a few steps to try to make sense of this.

Dakota sat on a table and picked up a Dawn comic book, as she did.

"Wow," she said, "what a lot of... dead things you've got here."

"I like natural history," Cesar said, without looking up from his undertaking.

"So do most serial killers," she replied.

Cesar chuckled.

Liv was still unsure if she wanted these two to like her. She picked up something right at hand, an Indian arrowhead bound, with sinew, to a long bone. She didn't see any obvious traces of blood, but she didn't want to examine it too closely. She dropped it and wiped her hands on her jeans.

Dakota snorted.

"What?" Liv snapped. "You help him hide the bodies?"

Dakota set down his comic book. "This is where I do business."

"Business?" It sounded like a lie he told himself to maintain his dignity, like when Dad referred to running out to do Grandma's shit chores as "going to work."

"Commerce," Dakota said, as if using different words made it less pathetic. "You know, *quid pro quo?*"

Not it was Liv's turn to snort. "What do you have that anyone would want to '*pro quo*'?

Dakota got down from the table and checked to make sure that there was no one lurking in the hall. He nudged her books inside with his foot and pulled the door shut.

Liv didn't worry too much about this. She was pondering which option would be best if the boys tried anything: the pepper spray in her pocket, or the bone and flint weapon already at hand.

Dakota went back to his table, pulled out a blue plastic folder that had been taped to the underside, and handed it to Liv. Inside, were all types of school forms: doctor's notes; hall passes; permission slips, and grade cards. Some already had forged signatures on them.

"Really?" was all she had to say.

"So what do you think?"

"It's a bunch of shit."

Dakota eyes went wide, and his lips pinched tight.

Cesar just snickered in the background.

Liv pulled out one of the completed slips and held it out for him.

"Most kids' parents learned handwriting in the nineties. This signature is pure Zaner-Bloser from the nineteen fifties."

"Huh?" Cesar's ears pricked up when she started talking technique.

Dakota was still sulking over her criticism.

"A proper parental signature is a scrawl that just flies off the wrist, with complete contempt for penmanship," she said, "and their children."

She picked up a pen and whipped out a quick duplicate of her mother's signature on the back of the form. She held it up for them to appreciate the credible, but illegible, scrawl.

Dakota looked impressed, in spite of his bruised ego.

Feeling like showing off, she then did her version of the principal's signature. Liv finished the show with the governor of California, Arnold Schwarzenegger.

Dakota's eyes lit up like a kid's on Christmas.

Cesar beamed at his pale little friend.

For the first time, Liv felt like she had nothing to be afraid of with these two.

"So, Liv," Dakota said, "would you be interested in a partnership?"

* * *

After Señor Vizcarra and his crew watched the Cunninghams disappear around the bend off the road on foot, he called out to his men:

"I have a very important job, men. I am looking for one volunteer."

Their ears all perked up, like good little dogs expecting a treat.

"I would like a show of hands," he continued, smiling like a happy father. "Who here has a girlfriend in town?"

All but the most ugly and uncivilized raised their hands. A lecherous chuckle passed among those with their hands up.

"Very good. Very good." Abraham Vizcarra nodded and smiled, but those who knew him well recognized the signs of trouble. "Now, for those of you with girlfriends, how many of them have young daughters?"

Several quickly dropped their hands, looking about to see who might still be in the boss's sights. A few, with limbs shaking, tried to drop below Vizcarra's watchful gaze. Only Gordo seemed unconcerned. He stood at the front of the group with his hand in the air, as hairy, dim, and fat as his name implied.

"Yes, you will do." Vizcarra pointed at Gordo, who smiled like an idiot from getting the attention.

"So what's the job, boss?"

Vizcarra jingled a set of car keys and a plastic cow key fob in his hand. They belonged to the rusty, busted blue pick-up they had just acquired at gunpoint. Coming up to Gordo, Vizcarra put an arm around the man's shoulders, while holding the keys in his other hand.

"There is an old military installation in the woods up that way." Vizcarra pointed the way from which the Cunninghams had come. He occasionally jangled the shiny keys to keep Gordo's attention.

"Uh-huh."

Vizcarra dropped the keys into his subordinate's greasy hand.

"I want you to drive the old couple's truck up there and ram it through the gates."

"Aren't they going to shoot me if I do that?"

Vizcarra dismissed the thought with wave of his hand and a carefree smile. "Nothing to worry about, old friend. The facility is mothballed... abandoned. There will be nobody there at all."

"If you say so."

"That's the way to be thinking, Gordo. Good work." Vizcarra began walking Gordo toward the pickup full of pot. "Once you are there, I want you to set fire to the truck. That should get our message across."

"What message is that, boss?"

Vizcarra stood face to face with Gordo and gripped his shoulders with both hands.

"You don't FUCK with Vizcarra."

"Oh, yeah. That message." Gordo nodded thoughtfully. This short conversation had just about taxed his reservoir of deep thought and words. "What do I do after that?"

Vizcarra grinned and clapped his hands on Gordo's upper arms.

"You go away."

"Huh."

Vizcarra stepped back and crossed his arms, his face neither happy, nor murderous. His men knew that he was poised to lash out in almost any direction.

All except Gordo. "What'd I do?"

Vizcarra shook his head, but remained calm. "A little bird has told me that you have been laying hands upon your girlfriend's fourteen-year-old daughter when Mama's away. That is not the kind of behavior I can condone."

"Who said—"

Vizcarra put a single finger to his lips.

Gordo shushed.

Nobody died in that general vicinity for the next few seconds, though the potential was there.

"If you do not want that little bird to be a vulture pecking out your last eyeball, you will do as I say. You will get into that truck. You will set it on fire and, when you are done, you will start walking until you find a place where nobody knows your ugly face. Or you die. Either ending would be satisfactory to me."

"This isn't fair," Gordo cried. "Whoever told you this, *patron*, was a liar!"

He took a step toward Vizcarra with his arms outstretched. He took two steps back from Gordo and off-handedly touched his own nose.

Every assault rifle and shotgun in the hands of his fellows came up to bear on Gordo. At this range, and in this number, the first barrage would turn him into soup.

Gordo held up his hands.

"You will leave with only what you have on your back. You may have whatever you like from the truck."

Gordo tried to protest without provoking the men with guns.

Vizcarra went on without taking notice.

"Your compatriots will dice for your clothing, as the Romans did with our Blessed Savior." Vizcarra crossed himself and then backed away. "Go, now."

Gordo had seen this happen often enough to know he had no choice, and only seconds to leave. Without saying goodbye, since any one of these men would be glad to shoot him in the face, he got into the truck and left forever.

TWO LAIRS

Dakota and Cesar followed Liv up the driveway to the side door everyone used. Drying squirrel hides on stretcher racks hung from the trees and swayed in the wind. Dozens of wind chimes tinkled away. Most had a bleached squirrel skull as the weight that made them swing in the breeze. Concrete squirrel garden ornaments in the front flowerbeds showed signs of small arms fire.

"So, this is it," Liv said as they stopped at the steps. "My scary great-grandmother's house."

"Has anyone come out of there alive?" Dakota asked. For a kid who hung out in a private museum of unnatural history, he took Grandma's yard decorations a little too much to heart.

"Where do you think I sleep," Liv snarked back, "the crawlspace?"

"Well, you're pretty scary, too," Cesar said. "So we figured you have a more than even chance of taking her on."

Liv smiled, in spite of her experience and world view. "I

believe that is the nicest thing anyone has said to me since we came to this Wi-Fi-forsaken shit hole."

Liv fished a latchkey out of her backpack as she and Cesar climbed the stairs. A lace curtain fluttered behind a window near the door and fell back into place.

Dakota, still down on the driveway, pointed at the door opening behind them with all the hinge-creaking of horror movie entrance. Great-Grandma Day stood in the doorway in sensible sweater and stretch pants. She held her shotgun in the crook of her arm.

"Back from school, and with friends," she rasped. "How nice."

"Hi, Grandma. These are my new friends—"

"I know who they are. Everybody knows everybody's business in a town this small," she said. "You boys gonna come in?"

Dakota fiddled with his fingers as he stood out of reach.

"I don't know, Mrs. Brodnansky gave us a lot of homework for tonight," he mumbled.

"I've got snacks," she crooned. "Cookies. Jerky. Lots of milk to wash it down with."

Cesar made a silent begging face.

Liv remained neutral as Great-Grandma looked her way with an expression of disappointment. "We even have raw vegetables."

"Well, cookies sound good," Dakota admitted. He began up the stairs.

Cesar made a silent celebratory gesture as Liv, and the old lady with the shotgun, went inside.

Dakota whispered harshly to his friend as he held the door. "You do remember the story of Hansel and Gretel, don't you?"

* * *

Squirrels waited for Gordo on the other side of the gates. He honestly didn't know why he ended up here. If he had a thought in his head, and the spine of an axolotl, he would have taken the truck and driven to the Gulf of Mexico, where his sister lived. But, *Patron* Vizcarra would not hesitate, for one second, to hand him over to the DEA, or the Sinaloans, or even that little bitch, Consuela's, family. So, like a good little dog whipped by his master, Gordo would do as he was told.

But he could have a little fun first.

The gates and fence stood eight feet tall, solid chain link with two-inch pipe frames. Razor wire coiled along the top of the fence. The government didn't want to make it easy for anyone trying to sneak in. The rusty white signs on the gates had a lot of words in English that Gordo didn't understand, but the phrase, *TRESPASSERS WILL BE SHOT*, was painfully familiar.

There weren't any guards to do the shooting, just those damn squirrels. Hundreds of the little bastards, all shapes and sizes, some of them as large as small dogs and black and tan, like Rottweilers.

Must be something atomic, thought Gordo, *a nuclear test ground full of mutant squirrels, like in the movies.*

He backed the truck across the dirt road, giving him the maximum straightaway of maybe twenty-five feet. Putting it in park, he took a moment to rifle through the glove box. There wasn't much of anything useful, just a twenty-two-caliber revolver with five rounds, and half a bottle of Bourbon.

He drained the bottle and tucked the pistol into his pants. Then, he flipped the truck into drive and rammed the gates. The gates flew wide as the truck hit them, in spite of the heavy chains and padlock. Like paddles on a pinball machine, they swung inward and swept the gathered squirrels to either side. As he drove onto the grounds, the squirrels rushed forward, some leaping up onto the hood, some falling beneath the wheels.

Gordo spun the truck in doughnuts. He could feel the bumps of little corpses under the tires, but they still covered the hood and windshield. No matter how fast, or wildly, he turned, the squirrels stuck like glue. It all stopped with a bone-braking crash as the truck plowed into a tree.

Gordo was dazed, his bleeding face coming to rest on the steering wheel. This truck was too old for a luxury like an air bag. He looked up enough to see the radiator steam where it was wrapped around the tree. Everything was pushed up, and to one side, from the way the truck tried to climb the trunk in its last moments.

Squirrels leapt back onto the crumpled hood and began to gnaw at the edges of the windshield. It had not shattered from the impact, but it was crisscrossed with fractures.

Gordo was never very good at decisions. With a mild concussion, and a half-bottle of Wild Turkey, in him, he decided to pull out his pistol and start shooting squirrels through the glass.

He may have killed five of them, but their brethren took advantage of the gaps left behind. They chewed at the edges of the holes, enlarging them and forcing their pointy little rodent faces through the glass. The first few came through like fat, furry rain drops passing through a leaky roof. Gordo struck out at them, with his bare hands, and his pen knife. It was like holding back the rain. One by one, the squirrels filled the truck's cab with fur, teeth, and blood.

Gordo's last thought was that he should have saved one of the bullets for himself.

THE SQUIRREL GUANTLET

The kids sat around the coffee table, eating jerky and carrot sticks. One of Grandma's documentaries on squirrel learning and behavior played on the seventy-two-inch TV, flickering like a drive-in movie in the dark.

The narrator explained the experiment: biologists wanted to see if electric shocks would deter squirrels from attempting the obstacle course to the feeder, or encourage faster learning. Liv figured that Grandma just liked seeing squirrels get electrocuted.

Dakota held up one of the bite-sized chunks of dried meat. "This tastes great! What is it, venison?"

"It's squirrel," Grandma called out from the kitchen.

Dakota dropped his jerky like it was on fire.

Cesar looked at his chunk, appraisingly, and then popped it into his mouth. Obviously, he didn't care that he was eating Teriyaki Rodent.

Liv shook her head and dipped a carrot stick in the bowl of Ranch dressing on the platter. She hoped there was no squirrel in that.

"The one trait that marks squirrels, the world over, is their persistence," the TV narrator intoned.

"And their chewiness," Dakota grumbled.

Grandma came in from the kitchen with a tray filled with glasses of milk, and a plateful of cookies.

"Here you go, a big, brimming glass of whole milk for each of you. Kids don't drink enough milk anymore."

"So says the dairy farmer trying to boost sales." Liv said this under her breath, but she wasn't overly concerned who heard it.

"How did you get so cynical?" Grandma asked, though it didn't sound like she disapproved. "I drink milk, and I watch things. It's what I do."

Dakota took one of the glasses and chugged milk to get the taste of seasoned dried squirrel's butt out of his mouth.

Cesar stuffed a cookie in his face and mumbled thanks between sips.

Liv took a cookie, what looked like an oatmeal raisin cookie, though she had her doubts. Dakota examined the dark spots on his cookie.

"Is there any squirrel in this?" he asked.

Before she could respond, something on the TV caught her attention. The old lady looked up and pointed at the screen. "You'll want to see this. It's the best part."

The camera tracked across a grassy obstacle course, filled with every anti-squirrel device considered humane: poles, taut cables, spinners, acrylic shields, and coiled springs. The last time they had watched this, Grandma had complained to Liv that they didn't use flame-throwers and sentry guns.

"Though declared to be totally squirrel-proof by its inventors," the narrator droned, "it took only two days for most subjects to solve this gauntlet of deterrents."

The kids, and Grandma, watched in grudging admiration as

the squirrel ran through its paces, like a fluffy ninja. At the end, it slid down over the top of the spinning birdfeeder to feast while hanging by its toes.

"Wow!" Cesar said as he took another cookie.

"Those damn little tree-rat bastards are just too smart for our own good," Grandma grumbled.

"Looks like," Dakota said.

"But I'd like to see them outsmart a butt-full of buckshot!"

"They're living beings," Liv said. "You can't just shoot everything you don't like."

Great-Grandma Day twisted her face up in a look of surprise and dismay. "Where do get your crazy ideas?" she snapped. "The Second Amendment protects my right to plug rodents of all stripes, coyotes, and cow-hugging potheads."

* * *

Ellen opened the back door to let Grover out into the backyard. As vapor-locked as any other Golden Retriever, he just stood there, sniffing circles in the grass, instead of doing what he'd been let out to do.

"Go do your business," she said in a much gruffer version of her radio voice. She might sound like hot sex on buttered toast to the dog, but that was only because she fed him. "Be quick about it. I've got a hot date tonight at the Indian Bingo Hall."

She normally kept an eye on him. Even though the hilly backyard was fenced in, it was far enough out in the sticks to make skirmishes with coyotes, or mountain lions, possible. Unfortunately, Ellen was running late, and she trusted that the powers above would watch out for her idiot dog.

Grover continued to sniff for the best place to relieve himself and advertise his presence to others.

A small, gray squirrel dashed across the grass to his left and leaped up to land on the lid of the battered old trash can. It looked down from the edge of the can, its tail flicking this way and that, like a semaphore flag.

The dog found this irresistible and leaped up, with its forepaws on one edge of the receptacle. The can came down toward him, with the lid falling one way, and the squirrel leaping the other. Grover took a moment to snuffle around in the trash that spilled out of the shiny steel can. All thoughts of the squirrel flew out of the retriever's tiny brain.

The squirrels had a longer attention span. Two Avenger Squirrels rushed up behind Grover and nipped at his haunches. This goosed him into the can and smashed his nose into the bottom.

Three more of the big black and tan rodents rammed the side of the trashcan, in unison, to send it slowly rolling down the hill. Grover gave out muted whimpers and yelps from the rolling container each time it hit a bump.

The Avenger Squirrels gave chase, like playful wolves scampering after a wounded caribou. The other squirrels sanitized the scene of the crime, dragging away loose trash, and the lid, where it could not be seen from the porch.

The back door opened again and Ellen shouted from inside. "Grover, you dim-bulb dog! I don't have time for this."

After about fifteen seconds of listening for her dog, she called out again, "All right, be that way. I'll see you in the morning."

She closed and locked the door as dozens of squirrels skittered through the bushes to join their brethren at the canine buffet at the bottom of the hill.

ROADKILL ENTERPRISE

D akota and Liv sat at a desk in their secret hideout.
Liv was whipping out forged hall passes.
Dakota was watching Liv make him a fortune. He
picked up one of the passes for inspection.

"You sign Miz Brodnansky better than she does," he said.

"She's easy," Liv replied, not raising her head from her work.
"Very tight, probably got As in penmanship in the nineteen-
sixties. Obviously signs of some mental issues."

Cesar came thumping into the room, carrying a large card-
board box that mostly blocked his line of sight. Even worse, it
originally held super absorbent sanitary pads.

"Couldn't get a really big, embarrassing box?" Dakota
quipped.

"Give me a break," Cesar muttered, "it was all I could find."

He looked excited when he was able to put down the box in
an empty spot.

"I think we may have hit the jackpot."

He opened the cross-folded lid and was nudged back by the wave of flies and a near-visible cloud of funk.

"It smells like a shit-pot." Liv sniffed and then gagged. She stood and took a few steps back with, a forgery-in-progress held across her lower face, like a dust mask.

"It's dead," Cesar stated matter-of-factly.

"If it smelled that bad, and it was still alive, I'd think about killing it."

Dakota pulled on a pair of black rubber gloves and a filter mask. He reached inside the carton and pulled out a ghastly collection of meat, fur, and bones. Stretched out to full length, tip of tan fluffy tail to fanged skull, it was nearly four foot long.

"What the hell is that thing?" Liv wheezed as she retreated to the furthest corner of the little room.

"I would say it's some kind of weasel," Cesar said, "though the feet look like something arboreal."

"Maybe, a pine marten."

"At that size? This is twice their normal size."

"Whatever it is, I'm sure Brodnansky is going to pay the big bucks for it."

"Wait a minute." Liv had taken to fanning the stink away from her face with her paper. "You sell roadkill to the science teacher?"

"You call it roadkill," Cesar said, "we prefer to think of it as a scientific curiosity."

Dakota gently folded it back into its napkin box. "Let's go see her right now."

* * *

Cesar held the door as Dakota took his turn to carry the box into the science lab. Both had on their gloves and kept their masks around their necks.

Liv followed a few paces behind to avoid looking interested. The sounds of frogs and splashing water at the front of the room showed where Ms. Brodnansky was preparing for the next period's dissections.

Her hair was piled up on the top of her head, like a steel-gray mass of cotton candy. With her black rubber gloves and apron, along with her safety goggles, she looked like a mad scientist's grandmother.

"Pithing frogs, Miz Brodnansky?" Cesar asked.

"Nothing like a good fresh bull frog, especially if you can still see the heart beating." She fished a palm-sized frog out of the big white bucket and held it, belly down, on the table.

The amphibian protested, with one raucous squawk, before the teacher drove a T-pin through its brain. The frog spasmed then went still.

Liv definitely wasn't interested in brain-dead frogs. She idly back-pedaled toward plants and specimens on top of the clunky, black, lab tables along the right wall. A pad-locked terrarium filled with rocks and sand caught her attention.

"So, Mr. Halverson, Mr. Carnicero." Brodnansky laid the pithed frog in a dissecting tray and extracted another victim from the bucket. "How are my two little naturalists this morning?"

"We've got something you're gonna love," Dakota said; he practically glowed.

The enthusiasm and avarice hurt Liv's eyes. She went back to the locked terrarium, where an engrave plaque read: *Crotalus horridus, Western Timber Rattlesnake.* A lone white mouse sat on the sand, surrounded by rocks and hidden serpents.

"Oh, Mickey," Liv groaned, "you're about to have a bad day."

She decided that she'd rather have a rematch with the dead thing in the box than watch feeding time.

Cesar put his mask back in place and opened the box.

Even Ms. Brodnansky, who spent her days with formaldehyde and middle-schoolers, was knocked back by the smell.

"I found this in the woods north of town," Cesar said, "near the abandoned army base."

Brodnansky twitched at the mention of the base.

Dakota and Cesar were too excited to notice.

She displayed an even bigger tell when Dakota laid out the mess of fur and bones on the lab table in front of her.

"We have no idea what it is," said Dakota, "but we hoped you would like it."

"What's wrong, Ms. Brodnansky," Liv asked sweetly. "You're not bothered by a dead whatever-it-is, are you?"

"Miss Day. I didn't see you lurking there in the shadows." Ms. Brodnansky composed herself instantly and smiled. "I'm not bothered, just... surprised. It is like nothing I've seen around these parts before."

Cesar and Dakota bumped fists.

"So it's worth a lot of money?" Dakota asked.

Brodnansky scrunched her face up to one side. "Yes, I would say so. Twice my usual rate: four dollars."

"Ten," Dakota shot back.

"That's awfully steep."

"It's an unusual specimen," Cesar countered. "An arboreal rodent with canines and incisors of a carnivore. Much larger than anything else in the neighborhood."

"A Rodent of Unusual Size," Dakota said.

"Exactly," said Cesar. "Maybe, the Natural History Museum in Eureka would be interested."

"My dad would be glad to drive us," Liv added.

Brodnansky grunted as she faced down the three young shake-down artists.

"Ten it is."

She bent down and retrieved her purse from beneath the lab table. After she pulled two fives from her wallet, she made as if to give them to Dakota, but pulled them from his grasp.

"You will wash your hands before you touch anything else," she declared. "Lord knows what parasites and pathogens are festering on that specimen."

The boys stripped off their gloves and washed up in one of the sinks.

Brodnansky fixed Liv with a wry grin. "I'm glad to see you taking an interest in science... and free enterprise. Let's keep this our little secret until we know what we have, okay?"

"Sure thing." Liv half-smiled. "And Dakota won't even charge you any extra for that."

Cesar returned to collect the money.

"Thank you very much. Pleasure doing business with you."

Ms. Brodnansky pulled over an illuminated magnifier to examine the corpse as the kids retreated to their secret hideaway.

* * *

In the hallway, Cesar waved the fives like a victory banner. "Like I said, jackpot!"

The boys fist-bumped and whooped.

Liv just shook her head. "Something smells worse than that dead thing we just sold her."

"What do you mean?" Dakota asked.

"Brodnansky knows way more about this than she's telling us."

Cesar looked at her, doubt mapped on his face. "How do you know?"

"You live through a divorce," Liv said, "you develop a skill set."

"At least you have parents," Cesar said with a frown. "Both of mine died two years ago."

"I'm sorry. Car wreck?"

"No, elevator accident."

THE VOICE

C hris ambled down the sidewalk of the main drag with a shopping bag in either hand.

Olivia, and a silver-haired Asian woman in a KILT sweatshirt, approached from the opposite direction.

They both smiled as they saw him.

"So," Olivia said, "you've given up on Crickson's dazzling nightlife?"

"Huh?" He had spent most of the day disassembling and refurbishing the pumping system, then Grandma's project for Burning Man. He wasn't exactly firing on all cylinders mentally.

Olivia pointed at the Redwood Video bag in his left hand.

"A night in with a bunch of videos?"

"Oh, yeah." He held up the bag slightly, as if he had just discovered it on the end of his arm. "Anything but squirrels. Did you know that there are over two thousand documentaries on squirrels?"

"And your grandmother has them all?"

"On a steady rotation, like a top 40 station."

The older woman pointed at the video store bag and spoke. The incredibly sexy Voice which read hog futures and obituaries, and had entranced Chris earlier, came out of her mouth. "Redwood Video is Crickson's best choice for home entertainment. They are friendly, economical, and have a very well-stocked adult section."

Chris went slack-jawed listening to her.

She bobbed her head from side to side and grinned. "That was part of their commercial on our station."

Chris slowly rose out of his fog of rosy-pink adulation for her.

"Y-You--- you're the Voice..."

The Voice and Olivia shared a chuckle.

"They all call me that."

"Maybe we should trademark that," Olivia said.

"Too late. That TV show one of the networks is bringing out, you know."

"Oh, yeah. Actually, we call her Ellen Park," Olivia told Chris. "Ellen, Chris."

The two of them shook hands.

Chris held on a little too long. "You don't look anything like what you sound," he said.

"And what should I look like?" she asked with a coy smile.

"Oh, I don't know," he sighed. "Tall, pale, willowy. Red hair blowing in the wind, you rising out of the sea on a giant scallop shell."

"I think we opened a window into your soul we should have left closed," Olivia said.

The words seemed to just bubble out of his mouth unmanaged, "Little naked cherubs fluttering around, singing your praises..."

"You're tired." Olivia patted his shoulder. "We'll talk later."

"Spoilsport." Ellen stuck her tongue out at Olivia.

She ignored her and leaned close to Chris. "Maybe, we could grab a bite sometime?" Olivia asked him. "Someplace without squirrels."

"Really?" The proposal bumped him out of his fugue state.

"Sure," she beamed. "It's been a while. A lot to catch up on."

"You could always stop by my place," Ellen purred. "I'll show you *my* extensive adult video section." She waggled her eyebrows at him.

He looked away to catch Olivia grinning wickedly.

"I've got to go," he muttered. He gave a half-hearted wave to Olivia. "I'll call you." He retreated, as quickly as possible, without sprinting.

Olivia and Ellen giggled like little girls once he disappeared around the corner.

"You are so bad," Olivia snorted. "He is young enough to be your son."

"Good. We can start with breast-feeding."

"Ellen!" Olivia shrieked.

"I get lonely. Since my dumb dog Grover ran away, I don't even have him to talk to."

Rafael pulled his SUV up to the twisted gates of the old Titan silo and parked it. He flipped on the flashing lights, painting the crash scene in reds and blues in the twilight. He wondered if there was anyone he should call before he set foot on federal land. Even though the *TRESPASSERS WILL BE SHOT* sign was on the ground with half the chain-link gate, some of these guys were serious.

Rafael muttered a few choice words in two languages and got out of the truck. He held his flashlight in his left hand. He rested his right hand on the butt of his service automatic, just in case.

The road just inside the gate was a bloody mess. Blood, fur, and gore were spread across the pavement. Bloody tire tracks marked grand circles that led to a battered blue pickup, wrapped nose-first around a tree.

Rafael took up the radio handset that hung at his shoulder as he slowly followed the tracks to the truck. "Kay, do you copy?"

"I'm right here, Rafael," she responded over the radio. "Whatcha got?"

"Found the Cunninghams' truck just inside the gates of the old missile base. Plowed right into a tree."

He moved carefully toward the front of the vehicle. He noticed that, though it looked like the driver had run over a few dozen small animals, there were no bodies.

"Any sign of the driver?" Kay asked.

He peered through the shattered windshield, shining his light over the glistening red surfaces; they looked to be coated with drying blood. A partial skeleton, its lower jaw fallen free of the skull, sat sideways behind the wheel.

"Most of him." *What the hell had Mr. Cunningham done to deserve this?*

"Messed up from the crash?"

Little bits of meat hung from the bones. It looked like a rack of ribs after a cookout.

"I don't think so," Rafael muttered. "You'd better send Sgt. Chuck with his crime scene kit, and a hook for the truck."

"Coming your way," Kay said. "Don't go wandering off until you have back-up."

"Copy that."

Though Rafael liked horror movies just as much as the next guy, this was a far scarier thing in *his* town, with people he knew, without special effects. He backed away from the crash, making his way to his truck. He was sure he'd feel a lot less rattled within arm's reach of his riot gun.

LAW & HORROR

Once Sgt. Chuck and Montoya had shown up with the crime scene truck, Rafael was able to seal off the area with black and yellow crime scene tape. They moved quickly, focusing on the task at hand. The scene was horrific, but Humboldt County regularly had grotesque incidents. Whether it was a farmer falling off his tractor and running himself over with his disc harrow, or a couple in an MG convertible hitting a four-hundred-pound wild pig, deaths often wound up being sudden, painful, and insanely messy.

Sluggo, in his denim vest and seed company cap, leaned on his tow truck outside the barrier. Not the brightest product of the Humboldt County education system, he wasn't at all curious about the forensic investigation, but he always was up to get a rise out of Rafael and Cpl. Montoya.

"Remember the good old days," the massive redneck drawled, "when we used to be worried about the Columbian cartels taking over?"

"I wouldn't exactly call those the good old days, Sluggo." Sgt.

Chuck grumbled as he dusted for fingerprints on the truck.

"Yeah," Sluggo went on, "but we don't have problems with Columbians anymore. The Mexicans killed and ate them all."

He nodded, knowingly, to Rafael. "No offense, Corporal Carnoceratops." Sluggo grinned as if it were a great trick coming off that stupid.

Rafael stood and squared off with the asshole, just out of arm's reach.

"Since my people all come from Guatemala, and fat, dumb white boys can't tell the difference," Rafael said with a shrug, "none taken."

Sluggo looked almost more hurt than angry. "No point in getting nasty," he snapped.

Rafael ignored Sluggo's pale, pained feelings. "Now, Corporal Montoya, her people, come from Matamoros, so you might convince her to eat you, but I think she's on a low-fat, high-IQ diet."

Sluggo dropped his arms to his sides, looking as if he was ready charge.

Rafael relaxed and set a hand on his police baton. He settled most of his weight on his back leg, putting himself in a good position to kick, punch, or swing.

Montoya, a few feet off, looked down through her camera, without taking any pictures.

"I think we have everything but the body bagged and tagged," Sgt. Chuck said as he appeared just behind Rafael's left ear. "Why don't we pack this up while Sluggo gets back in his truck and does his job without saying anything stupid?"

The sergeant was big enough to seriously kick Sluggo's doughy ass, which was why the other two got most of the attention. The tow truck driver nodded quietly and got back in the cab.

"Yes, sergeant." Montoya fell to packing out.

Sgt. Chuck looked down on Rafael steadily, able to see the top of his head without stretching. "Is there a problem with that?"

Rafael relaxed his combat stance. "No, Chu—"

The sergeant cut him off with a warning glance.

"No, Sergeant Slaybaugh. No problem at all, sir."

"That's the kind of spirit I like to hear."

Rafael and Montoya collected up the evidence bags, tape, and equipment as Sluggo fired up his truck to maneuver it into position. In less than ten minutes, the tow truck had the pickup pulled clear of the tree.

As Sluggo finally reached the front of the truck to see if he could wedge a dolly in place for towing, he also got a quick look inside the cab. He went green and slack-jawed at the sight.

Sgt. Chuck came up beside him with a tight grin on his face. "Do you have any more ugly, tasteless remarks to make while we try to figure out which one of the Cunninghams got eaten alive?"

Sluggo shook his head minutely. "We're going to need a flatbed," he said as he retreated to the radio in his cab.

"That's all right," Sgt. Chuck called out. "We still have to wait for the coroner's van before we can go anywhere!"

* * *

From her squirrel-mounted cameras in the trees, the Sciuriologist was able to see the entire operation. Three black SUVs pulled up to the Abernathy's plot, southwest of the federal lands. Eight or nine grim looking men in black DEA windbreakers tumbled out of the vehicles. They moved at a relaxed pace, as if to a picnic, except they held tools and fuel cans in their hands.

Stacks of drying marijuana plants waited for them just inside the tree-line, away from the prying eyes of drones and heli-copters. The DEA agents dragged them into the center of the clearing and dowsed them with gasoline.

One of them, his jacket conveniently marked *Chief*, ambled up to the bonfire. He pulled a NORML flier from his pocket, set it alight and pitched it into the stack. The gasoline, given a few minutes to evaporate, caught with an impressive "whoomph" sound. The entire crop burst into flame within seconds.

One of his subordinates wiped the back of hand across his forehead.

"That's the third field we torched this week. They're like cockroaches. You step on one, and two more appear."

"You step on enough of them," the chief said, "and they'll go someplace else."

The wind shifted, and the billows of thick gray smoke swung around to envelop the agents. He side-stepped the cloud and waved his team to follow.

"Okay, people, moved upwind," he shouted. "I don't want you getting the munchies and cleaning out the local Seven-Eleven."

In the canopy around the clearing, several hundred squirrels, of various genotypes took in the clouds of cannabis. The Sciuri-ologist could monitor their vitals on the screens before her. At first, the smoke irritated the squirrels but, then, it had a mellowing effect. Blood pressures and resting pulses dropped, and a definite wobble showed in the Monitor Squirrels' video feed.

Even the normally high-strung Avenger Squirrels chilled in the branches. The normally frenetic Sappers and Runners laid draped over branches like limp fur tippets. The wind shifted again, and the rodents' vital signs slowly returned to normal.

As they did, the squirrels grew restive. Their slurred chirps and clicks indicated that their blood sugar was dropping and the munchies were setting in. The squirrels went on the move.

They leaped from branch to branch, though not gracefully. Several missed their landings and plummeted down through the canopy. The Sciuriologist was treated to a Squirrel POV video of that when one of the Monitor Squirrels overshot its target. The continuing sine wave displays for heart and respiration showed that the squirrel had survived the fall, no doubt protected from injury because of its over-relaxed state.

The leaping rodents came to a stop as forest gave way to open pasture. A few dozen black and white dairy cattle grazed languidly on the knee-high grass. They looked too appetizing to resist.

The various breeds of squirrels descended the tree trunks, like a fluid flowing downhill. They pooled on the ground below and then made the rush toward the beef on the hooves. The domesticated cattle were too slow-witted to notice the threat until squirrels nipped at their heels. Only then did they run, and the killer squirrels pursued.

The rodents spread out like a carpet of fur and sharp teeth to sweep over the hindmost of the herd. Three of the cattle went down beneath the assault and, within minutes, were stripped to the bone.

The Sciuriologist chuckled to herself as her black-gloved hands played across the controls of her sensor controls. Pulse, respiration rate, blood pressure and sugar, even video, they all told a detailed story. It was an epiphany.

"Of course," she murmured, "the endogenous cannabinoid pathways are overstimulated by the THC in the smoke."

She smiled as she saw her hungry rodent-children bring down the fifth cow of the herd.

"It will be the perfect catalyst for my final assault."

PIECE OF TAIL

The sign on the chain-link fence around the Sheriff's impound lot declared, *NO TRESPASSING. VIOLATORS WILL BE SHOT AND FED TO THE DOGS.*

Dakota and Cesar ignored it as they peeled open the gap in the fence.

Liv was simply unimpressed.

The boys, acting like young gentlemen, held up the chain-link fabric to allow Liv to cross under first.

"Are we even supposed to be in here?" she asked.

"It's okay," Dakota said, "his uncle will vouch for us."

"That actually means 'no,' " Cesar said and looked sideways at his friend, "so keep your head down."

The three of them scuttled away from the fence near the tree-line, bent at the waist, and moved into the ten-acre lot filled with gravel, trash, and jailed cars. The cops parked the crappiest cars near where the kids came through. The newer cars, like the odd Porsche, or Cadillac that needed the most police protection, sat nearest the pre-fab office under the street light. Dakota frog-walked deeper into the shadows.

"Why are we heading this way?" Liv asked. When Dakota invited her along on their expedition into the impound lot, she thought they were after hubcaps, or spare parts, maybe even the platinum out of catalytic convertors. All the good stuff was under the lights.

Cesar clicked together the jaws of his green plastic forceps with a grin.

"Out-of-state vehicles bring in exotic specimens on their grills and windshields."

"We extend our collection range," Dakota added, "without having to pay for gas."

The boys scuttled over to a Lincoln Town Car with Louisiana plates and removed a fairly large praying mantis from the grille.

"Now, there's a beauty!" Cesar whispered as he put it into the empty plastic pickle jar he carried.

Dakota carefully documented the specimen with his pad and pencil.

"He's missing a couple of legs," Liv observed.

"We'll give Brodnansky a discount," Dakota replied.

They worked their way down the line of parked cars, pulling specimens out of the radiators, windshield wipers, and other nooks and crannies. Liv figured they collected seventeen moths, twelve variations on grasshoppers, a fistful of beetles, and a shrike. That was a tiny hawk, no bigger than Dakota's which that had gotten jammed into the space between a New Mexico El Camino's hood and windshield.

A battered and bloodied pickup truck was parked in the farthest and darkest corner, surrounded by police caution tape, and giving off an aura absolutely irresistible to the boys.

SQUIRREL APOCALYPSE • 63

"Wow, would you look at that," Dakota murmured. He started moving forward, as if drawn by magnets.

"Don't even think about it," Cesar snapped. "That is a crime scene!"

"Maybe we should go." Liv was a little anxious about all the officers who weren't at the sheriff's impound lot. Sooner or later, they would get done with filching free food at the local McDonald's and they would come back and catch her with these two idiots.

Dakota kept drifting toward the truck, slipping down on his hands and knees to look under the front bumper.

"Hang on, I think I see something down here..."

"It's not worth it," Cesar muttered.

"Just a second."

Dakota was at the front of the truck, staring at a black and tan furry tail hanging down from the engine compartment. He tugged on it with one hand, but it stayed put.

"This is a dumber idea than usual," Liv hissed through clenched teeth.

"I almost have it." He clamped on both hands and put his back into it.

Something came loose. Dakota fell flat on his back, with another black and tan dead thing smacked across his chest. This specimen was fresher, and smelled worse. Its entrails leaked across Dakota's black Batman T-shirt.

"Jesus H. Christ on a pogo stick," he shouted.

"What?" Liv snapped back.

"My Dad used to say that," Dakota said. "When Mom would call him up about child support."

Cesar helped his friend to his feet and then slapped him across the back of the head. "*Pendejo*."

Dakota grimaced and held the dead animal up along his arm.

From its nose, to tip of its tail, it was almost as long as the entire span of his arms.

"What do you think, five feet?" Dakota beamed, like he had landed a world-record fish.

"Give or take," Cesar muttered. He pulled back the animal's lips with the tips of his forceps. "Same dentition as the last specimen. This could be a brand new species."

"We have hit the big time!" It looked like they would exchange high fives, except Dakota had his hands full.

"Only you two would get this excited over road kill," Liv said. "I need to get new friends."

Dogs starting barking at the far side of the lot.

The boys both swiveled their heads in the direction of the sound.

"Uh-oh," Dakota said. "Time to go!"

"*Vamanos!*" Cesar collected up his specimens and evacuated toward their improvised exit.

Dakota fell in right behind them, trying not to swing his dead whatever too much.

"Nobody said anything about dogs!" Liv was too pissed to run yet.

"I thought we'd discuss it as the subject came up," Cesar yelled over his shoulder.

Liv took off running then, not sure if it was away from the dogs, or after these two idiots. She was about twenty feet away from the gap in the fence when the dogs came around corner. There were three of them, scarred-up, gnarly-looking mongrels that showed mostly teeth and gums as they closed in.

Liv sped up.

Dakota and Cesar did, too.

Dakota's prize cadaver was pummeling his right side as he

ran, spattering guts and fluid with each hit. Its yellow, sharp teeth seemed to be nipping at his ankles as he went.

Cesar got to the fence and peeled up one side of the cut chain link.

Dakota got the other side.

Liv silently thanked her father for all those stupid little league games he forced her to play as she slid, feet-first, for home through the breach.

Cesar came through right after her and got his pliers ready to cinch up the wire fence once Dakota came through.

The dogs were less than ten feet away when Dakota dove for safety, but he hung in space, like a marionette. Three or four of the freshly cut wires snagged the back of his black T-shirt. Dakota flailed and screamed, trying to reach behind his back to free himself.

Liv and Cesar did their best to reach in and unsnag him. His flailing just made things worse.

He still clutched their dead prize in his other hand. It swung from side to side, like a chew toy.

The dogs couldn't resist that. As they thundered up to the fence around Dakota, they sank their teeth into the roadkill instead of his one leg which was still within their reach.

Dakota used both hands to maintain his hold on the tail as the dogs worried at the body. It made a tearing sound as they shook their heads.

Cesar scooped double handfuls of gravel from the ground and flung it at the dogs. He kept up a steady stream of what Liv thought were obscenities in Spanish as he went. That had more effect than the gravel.

"Idiots!" Liv snapped. She put one hand in the middle of Dakota's back, pushing down as she lifted the chain link with her other.

He tore free with several gashes in his sweatshirt.

She wrapped her arms around his chest and pulled with all her strength.

The tail snapped off of the dead whatever. Liv and Dakota fell on their asses.

As Cesar pulled the gap in the fence closed to knit it together, the impound dogs shredded the black and tan corpse.

Liv wriggled out from under Dakota's bulk and dropped his head into the dirt.

Cesar rewired the gap in less than a minute and set his forehead against the fence as he watched the dogs fight for the biggest piece of his biological prize.

"Damn."

Dakota came up behind his best friend and laid a sympathetic hand on his shoulder. "At least you got a piece of tail."

Cesar sullenly took the chunk of black fur and bone.

"That's all my cousins from Vacaville seem to care about," Dakota said.

Liv dusted off her knees, and backside, and started off to where they had stashed her great-grandma's golf cart. She stopped a few yards down the trail when the boys didn't follow.

"You two are idiots," she said.

Cesar looked at the dead animal's tail he clutched in his hands. "You know, I think she's right."

Dakota clapped him heartily on the shoulder and put on his *It could be worse* expression.

"Hey, we've still got a lot of specimens!" Dakota grinned, but Cesar wouldn't respond. "We might even get Brodnansky to pay for just the tail!"

Cesar groaned and shook his head. "Come on," he said. "I want to go home."

PENCIL-THIN MUSTACHE

S herriff Maxwell was pouring herself a cup of coffee at the back counter as Rafael came in. It was a grey drizzly morning, and he was feeling the same way: just one too many Cuervos while watching TV last night.

"Carnicero," she said with a nod as she took her *Humboldt County Fair* mug back to her desk and ergonomic chair.

"Morning, sheriff," he replied, noncommittal.

She looked at him over the top of her mug with the slightest gleam in her eye. Rafael prepared himself for some attack on his mental equilibrium.

"Anything new with your nephew, corporal?" Her voice did not sound like butter would melt in her mouth.

"Excuse me?"

"Any teeth marks in his ass?" Her expression seemed to say, *Mind if I put a few in yours?* She had a reputation around town as a bit of a cougar, but she had always avoided fouling the chain of command with extracurricular activities.

"Someone broke into the impound lot again," she continued, "riled up the dogs."

"I'll have a word him." He would also have a word with Olivia and her delinquent son. Cesar had been a straight arrow honor student until the two of them started hanging out together.

"Makes no never mind to me," the sheriff said. "The dogs need their exercise, but the county can't afford any lawsuits."

"I understand."

"Good. If you decide you need to tie him down and spank him, I could give you a few pointers."

Sheriff Maxwell was in a particularly feisty mood this morning. Rafael looked back at her without blinking, a response that kept this just a mildly strange conversation instead of a sexual harassment case. He veered toward the coffee which he so desperately needed.

"Malcolm and I raised three boys ourselves," she said, "before I divorced him over the Krispy Kreme hostess."

Rafael sugared up his coffee and took a long draw, feeling the caffeine slap his brain cells into marching order. After another sip or two, he felt ready to get down to business.

"Anything more on the Cunninghams' truck?"

Maxwell rolled her eyes.

"They still say their truck was stolen while it was parked at the Lucky's. They have no idea who that mangled corpse behind the steering wheel might be."

"Of course." Rafael chuckled. "They're perfectly innocent and don't know a thing."

"Like every soul in San Quentin," she said. "We'll keep asking around, though, considering the state of the body, my first guess is—"

"Mexicans?"

Her smiled pinched up, as if she tasted something sour. She

SQUIRREL APOCALYPSE • 69

had had a long conversation with Sgt. Chuck about Sluggo last night.

"Violent drug smugglers of no specific ethnicity," she replied. "With something as sick as that, I want to arrest the right people the first time, if you know what I mean?"

"I hear you," said Rafael. "Thanks."

"Nothing to thank me for, doing my job the right way." She reached over to her in box and pulled out a thick sheaf of yellow phone messages. "Seems we got ourselves a buttload of animal calls over the weekend."

"Coyotes eating cats, again?"

"Cats, dogs, sheep, cattle, emus. Did you know that Doug Foulk had a bunch of emus?"

Rafael shook his head, not even sure what an emu was.

"The number of calls we've gotten," she said, "you'd think the coyotes would be causing traffic jams on the interstate."

"Might be cougars, too," Rafael said.

The sheriff looked at him for a moment, as if that were some kind of personal accusation, and then pushed on.

"Just this morning, got a call from Iris Day. Her grandson found a bunch of dead cattle on her property. The Walps were leasing the pasturage."

"A bunch?" Rafael heart fluttered, but he went back to his poker face. "What takes down a bunch of cattle all at once?"

"Don't know. You go talk to your old friend and see what he has. If it's nothing obvious, we'll put in a call to the state vet, or the ag extension."

"I got it." Rafael collected up his gear to go out on the call.

"I know you're mad at him for running out on you," the sheriff said.

"Who says that?"

"Everyone who remembers you three from twenty years

ago. Like that time some unknown miscreants filled every keyhole in Earl's Bait and Gun with epoxy putty." She scoffed. "Three little devils with one brain, that's what we used to say. I don't want anyone getting shot in my county, unless it can be justified."

Rafael checked his service automatic, and his spare magazine, on his Sam Browne belt. "No one needs to worry about that, ma'am."

* * *

Even though Chris stood on the other side of the aluminum cattle gate, the deputy in the county SUV chose to set off a little "whoop" of the siren to announce his arrival. Chris unchained the twelve-foot gate and swung it outwards to let him pass.

The driver pulled through the gate, head straight ahead, eyes concealed behind silver shades. It looked like Rafael drew the short straw to get this call, and he was going to take it out on Chris.

Chris secured the gate; he didn't want any of the Walps' surviving cattle getting loose. He then jogged up to the driver's side window. It rolled down a few seconds after he got there.

"Thanks for coming down," Chris said, "Grandma lost her shit when I told her about this."

"Just doing our jobs, sir." Rafael pulled a pen and notepad from his pocket. "So where's your dead cow?"

"Up on the other side of that row of hay bales." Chris pointed to the far side of the pasture, near the tree line. The other cows were avoiding that half. "But there's more than one."

"How many, do you think?"

"I don't know." Chris started feeling queasy again.

Rafael took off his glasses to display a look of bald contempt.

Chris cringed at that, but at least Rafael had gotten past pretending he was invisible.

"How the hell do you not know how many?"

"They're not my cows," Chris snapped back.

Rafael sucked on his teeth, making the same squeaking noise he used to make while plotting schemes back in the old days.

"And they're behind the bales?" he asked.

"Yeah."

"Let's take a look, then."

Rafael slid on his shades and rolled up the window as Chris jogged around to the passenger side. Just as he was reaching for the door, Rafael put the SUV in drive and nudged across the pasture at a walking pace.

Chris stood there, breathing in exhausts fumes and waiting for Rafael to stop.

He didn't.

Chris sprinted after him and came even with the door.

Rafael sat behind the wheel and stared straight ahead, as if he were on a Sunday drive.

Chris considered making a leap for the door, but his chances of falling beneath the wheels seemed high. It even seemed likely that Rafael would back up to finish him off. So, instead, he jogged alongside the green and white Sheriff's SUV, like a Dalmatian pacing a fire engine.

He was a little winded when they came to the hay bales. These were the six-foot tall plastic-wrapped type that gave him something cushy to lean against as he caught his breath.

Rafael got out and approached the remains spattered across the grass. As he walked, he tapped out a rhythm on his notebook with his pen, steadily, like a metronome.

The ankle-high grass was laid flat, as if run down by a truck from the tree-line thirty feet away to the six corpses at their feet. Each body had been split opened and devoured, most sections stripped down to bone and gristle. The hides had been shredded and scattered. Drying blood coated everything, and clouds of black flies fed on all of that.

"God, what a mess," Rafael said, somewhere between disturbed and impressed.

Chris came up behind his right shoulder. "You ever see anything like this before?"

"Predators kill livestock all the time." Rafael scratched out his initial notes. "It's the cost of doing business."

Chris nudged the nearest denuded skull with the tip of his shoe; he couldn't find a stick to prod it with.

"I understand that, but this is like they got attacked by piranhas. Even the bones got chewed."

Rafael gave him another one of those looks. "You watch a lot of *CSI*? Maybe *Wild Kingdom*?"

"What? Because I'm a city kid, I can't tell these poor animals have been stripped down to the bones?"

Rafael frowned and shook his head. "The top predators bring down an animal, and then the smaller predators and scavengers take their turn," he said. "It doesn't take that long for them to clean up a cow."

"Okay, give me a second." Chris had finally hit his limit. He pulled out his phone and started up the UdderTime app. Hopping carefully over piles of grue and wet leather, he got over to one of the ear tags that still remained, though most of the ear did not. He wiped the blood off the backside and scanned the VR code into the app.

"Ah-Hah!" Chris shouted as he held up the displayed info on his seven-inch screen. He then realized Rafael couldn't read it at two or three yards. He hopscotched back across the bloody grass to stick his phone under the deputy's nose.

"This is a program the Walps use to track their cows' milking schedule. This cow was last milked at six-thirty. That is certainly not enough time for your circle of life bullshit, unless we have hyenas I haven't seen before?"

"Okay." Rafael tapped and nodded. "Okay. We'll look into this. Have you seen any unusual people, or animals, around the farm in the last few days?"

"Yeah. There's this guy who used to be my best friend who's turned into a total asshat."

Rafael cocked his head to one side as he opened the notebook, "Asshat? Are you sure that's the term you want use right now?"

"*Bendejo?*" Chris offered. He wasn't sure how he could wedge *Chinga su madre* into the conversation.

"*Pendejo*," Rafael corrected. "Do you even know what that means?"

"It means "crazy person." Mom's housekeeper told me that."

"It means 'asshole.' Literally, it translates as 'pubic hair.' "

Chris was impressed with the scholarship, but he wasn't going to stop flogging this eviscerated cow of an argument.

"Oh, I'm *sorry*, I called you 'public hair' without realizing it." Chris ladled on the sarcasm, the way they used to as kids. "I might feel it appropriate to call you 'eyebrow' or 'armpit hair' or, even, 'pencil-thin mustache'..."

Chris paused for effect as Rafael fought not to smile.

"But I never meant to call you 'pubic hair.' "

The two of them stared each other down, daring the other to laugh first.

After about thirty seconds of facial twitches and strangled snorts, Chris broke into laughter first, the way he always had.

It was contagious, though, and Rafael joined in until both of them folded over.

They slowly regained their composure in the field amidst the partial carcasses.

"All right," Chris finally snorted. "What the HELL did I do to you that got you so pissed off? I haven't been in the same goddamned *state* the last twenty years."

Rafael worked his mouth and throat as if he were going to speak, but then just shook his head. "It's complicated."

"It's complicated? Complicated? My, what a refreshing change from my life of divorce, betrayal, and single parenthood amongst the squirrel-addled senior citizens of Humboldt County."

Rafael shrugged apologetically, but said nothing. He began tapping on his notepad again. Chris closed his eyes and sighed. "Okay, let's get back to something simple. What the hell kills six cows and chews them down to the bones in just one night? Aliens? Army ants? The all-you-can-eat crowd from Golden Corral?"

"I have no fucking idea."

"But you've seen things like this before, right?"

Rafael shook his head vigorously. "I haven't seen horror movies as bad as this."

Chris puffed out his cheeks and exhaled. "Whatever did this could probably eat every cow in Crickson and come back for our kids."

"That's exactly what I was thinking." Rafael was beginning to look a little shaky. The same as Chris, his kid was his weak spot.

"So," Chris finally said, "you got any scientists in town?"

LAB ACCIDENT

C hris felt openly dubious as they entered Brodnansky's darkened lab.

"I was hoping for someone with slightly better credentials than local high-school science teacher," he told Rafael.

"Janene Brodnansky worked with the state Fish and Game department for a couple of decades," Rafael replied. "After she retired, she decided to go into teaching to keep from going crazy, unlike certain other residents."

"My grandmother is a visionary."

"Sure."

The two of them crept up quietly on her as she spoke to three of her students at the front of the class. As they reached a padlocked terrarium filled with rocks and rattlesnakes, Rafael froze, staring at the back of the dark-haired boy's head.

Chris could see in the dim light of the lab that Liv and Olivia's son, Dakota, were the other two.

The rattlesnakes went off, perhaps sharing Rafael's venomous mood, or perhaps trying to warn Cesar of danger. The distinctive noise caught the attention of the teacher and students.

Cesar, holding what looked to be a black and tan animal tail, turned and caught sight of the two of them. The boy's eyes went wide, and he quickly passed the fur over to Dakota.

Liv and Dakota stepped back, as they caught the angry expression on Rafael's face.

Ms. Brodnansky, looking like Frankenstein's mother-in-law with her silver beehive and white lab coat, practically beamed as she saw her new visitors.

"Corporal Carnicero, Mr. Day. What a pleasant surprise!"

"It's been a day for surprises, Ms. Brodnansky." Rafael didn't take his eyes off of his nephew as he spoke. "I was very surprised to find out that someone had broken into the impound lot last night. Cesar, you wouldn't have any other revelations on that incident?"

The boy stood frozen, staring up at his uncle with the gun on his hip. His lips barely moved when he finally spoke. "Do we have to talk about this right now, Tio Rafael?"

"No. We can talk about this when I get home. We can talk about this over dinner. I'm sure we'll have a chance to talk about this a few times before bedtime."

"Yes, sir."

"Now, don't you have someplace else to be this period?"

"Yes," Cesar whispered. "Goodbye, Tio Rafael."

He rushed down the lab to the back entrance. Papers flew off the counters by the wake of his passing whoosh.

"We'd better get going, too," Dakota mumbled.

He and Liv made as if to follow Cesar, but Rafael inclined his head questioningly.

Dakota pointed toward the front door and then followed his finger.

Liv backed that way, waving awkwardly. "See you later, Dad."

As the two doors closed and fluttering papers settled to the floor, Brodnansky fixed Chris and Rafael with a look of bemusement.

"I suppose you two didn't come in for an impromptu parent-teacher meeting."

A silent exchange passed between Rafael and Chris, reminiscent of their old shenanigans:

This is a really stupid idea. Are you sure about this?

No. Let's see how bad it could get!

"We have a problem," Rafael muttered.

"Evidently." Brodnansky polished up her wire-rim glasses and perched them back on the bridge of her nose. "Is there anything I can help with?"

"I hope so." Chris sighed. "Something's eating our livestock."

Brodnansky chuckled without humor. "I've heard the rumors. Do you have anything for me to look at?"

Rafael laid out a folder of crime scene photos on the black countertop in front of her. She clucked to herself as she looked over the dead cattle, sheep, and emus. The corpse in the Cunningham's truck was still a classified part of an ongoing investigation and was left back at headquarters.

"Something has a very big appetite," she said.

Chris indicated the photos of the five, or six, cows on his grandmother's land. "What you see here, it happened in only a few hours."

"Impressive."

"And, whatever it is," Rafael added, "it has happened over a dozen times in our county."

Ms. Brodnansky contemplated the carnage in front of her. "This must be very unsettling to our neighbors. Terrifying, even."

"The other deputies have been reporting that some farmers are camping out in their fields with shotguns. Friendly fire could cause as much bloodshed as these predators."

Brodnansky began sorting the pictures, placing them in stacks that made no sense to Chris. She bit her lip as she looked over them again.

"May I have these for a while, Cpl. Carnicero?"

"Sure, these are digital copies. You can keep them. I'll let you know if we unearth anything else."

"You do that," she said as she fell to studying them under an illuminated magnifier.

"Later, then," Rafael said, already on his way out the lab's back door.

Chris wheeled around to catch up, flinching only a little bit when the rattlers started up making noises in their padlocked cage.

* * *

Chris rushed to catch up with the corporal, who marched through the hustle and bustle of class change. Rafael's jaw was set, evidently grinding away at some nagging problem, either the livestock deaths, or his nephew.

"So, what do we do now?" Chris asked, jostled by one middle-schooler after another.

"Brodnansky will get to work on her research. I have to go back on patrol," Rafael stated. "You can go feed your cows."

"They are not my cows!"

"Whatever." Rafael walked on without slowing.

Chris fell back for a few steps, then sprinted ahead to come up even. "You know I'm competent. I can contribute here," Chris shouted at Rafael's back.

"You've been doing wonders."

"Have you gone back to being an asshat?"

"Never stopped." Rafael hit the double doors and powered through. "*Pendejo.*"

Chris stopped in the doorway to yell at his old friend as he walked down the stairs to his county SUV. "Pencil-thin mustache!"

SOMEWHAT HOSTILE TAKEOVER

I t had only taken a couple of days for John Cunningham to get a new truck, though he had to get it from Bohannon's Pay & Drive. It was old enough to vote, only a few months from being allowed to drink, but it had four wheels and a working engine.

John and Mandy were on their way to their second site on the federal lands around the old missile silo. With a bit of luck and good weather, it would make up for all they lost to Vizcarra and his gang.

As they navigated a long, downhill curve on the dirt road, the twenty-gallon plastic jugs of water and fertilizer slid the entire length of the truck's bed. They slammed against the back of the cab to make a racket, like drunken men wrestling to fit through the slider glass in the back.

Both of them flinched and cranked their heads around at the sound. Neither of them had really recovered from the day when Vizcarra took their crop and their truck at gunpoint, or the interview with Sheriff Maxwell when they saw what had been done in the old truck. They had seriously discussed getting out of the business and moving south.

"Just another couple of weeks," he said, "and we'll be ready to harvest."

"From your mouth to God's ears."

John chuckled as he pulled the truck up to their plot and put it in park. "Trust me, we've earned a little bit of good luck with what we've been through."

He got out and dropped the tailgate. The two of them began pulling out the water jugs to help the crops make it through the next few days without rain. They had just emptied the jugs and put them back into the bed of the truck when they heard the sound of approaching engines.

"Good luck, huh?" Mandy drawled.

John did not take time to snipe back at her. He was already behind the wheel.

Mandy slammed the tailgate shut and leaped into the shotgun seat. Grasping the Jesus Strap with her right and pulling the door shut across her body with her left, Mandy held on for dear life. The new truck's rear end shimmied like a pole-dancer's as John put it onto the rutted dirt track. The other trucks were driving in the direction they had come. Their only escape was going even deeper into the federal land.

John ran the dirt trail as fast as the truck would stand it, steering as much with the brake and shifter as the wheel. A few of the plastic jugs bounced out right over the top of the bed, and Mandy found herself airborne on a few hills.

They came into the cathedral clearing, a widening of the dirt trail that was surrounded, on both sides, by pine trees as tall as a church spire, and it looked as solid as a stone wall. John was about to floor it through that straightway when he saw the trucks blocking the road ahead of them.

"Oh, shit!"

He clenched his jaw and pulled on the emergency break, sliding the truck into a sideways stop across the road. Amazingly, they did not flip end over end during their attempt.

He laid his hand on his chest as he tried to slow down his breathing. The terror of the short drive was almost enough to pop the seal on his last bypass.

"I put the truck between you and them," he gasped. "Get out your side, and go into the woods."

"No, John, that's a stupid idea." She rested her hand on top of his. "Besides, how far do you think *I'm* gonna be able to run?"

They sat in the cab, with only the sound of the Voice reading the hog futures, and they tried to settle down as the cloud of dirt the truck had raised slowly settled, too. Once the air was clear, the doors on the blockading trucks opened. Out stepped Vizcarra and his armed menagerie.

In his dark glasses and light linen suit, the drug lord looked like he was boarding a yacht instead of walking into an armed confrontation. He puffed on his cigar as he walked the thirty yards between them. His only concern seemed to be the quality of the tobacco and the beauty of the scenery. As he stepped up to John's side of the truck, he signaled for them to roll down the windows.

The other men, who carried automatic weapons, were not concerned enough to be pointing them at the Cunninghams' heads just yet.

As the glass came down between them, Vizcarra smiled broadly. "Mr. and Mrs. Cunningham, it is so nice to see you." He waved at the surrounding trees with his right hand. His cigar left spiral trails of smoke in the air. "I think this is a perfectly lovely place to discuss our new business arrangements. Would you please step out of the truck?"

* * *

Abraham Vizcarra had lit his second Havana about the time his men had brought the Cunninghams' crop in their trucks. The plants still had many of their roots attached, and the bundles were sloppily tied. They wouldn't need to hold together through much shipping.

The husband stared dumbly at the proceedings as his men piled the plants in the middle of the road. The woman, she knew right away. She fought against Esteban's grip, and he was none too gentle.

"Why don't you let her go?" Mr. Cunningham said. "I'm the one that makes all the business decisions."

Vizcarra came up to him slowly, making no sudden movements that might cause even more agitation for any parties involved.

"Oh, but yours is a family business, a mom and pop shop. We must have all the interested parties present for negotiations.

Mrs. Cunningham did not allow herself to be soothed. She struggled to free herself from his underling while she practically screamed at Vizcarra. "That's everything we have left in the world! Why don't you assholes just leave us alone?"

Esteban took offense at her tone. He twisted her arm behind her back and pressed her down onto her knees.

"*Puta*! You won't talk like that to us. We're the ones in charge here."

No doubt, Esteban would have said more, but Vizcarra was having no more of that.

He closed the space between them in three swift strides and slapped Esteban sharply across the cheek. He didn't use enough force to do any real damage, but it did catch his attention immediately.

"No more!" Vizcarra snapped. "We are not animals. Not like El Gordo. You do remember what happened to him?"

Esteban released Mrs. Cunningham quickly and stepped back.

Vizcarra gave him a bland, questioning look.

Esteban bobbed his head and turned to the old woman. "I'm sorry for my language, ma'am, and my behavior. I hope you will accept my apology."

Mrs. Cunningham only glared at him.

Vizcarra dismissed him with a wave of his hand and helped her to her feet.

She pulled herself from his grasp as soon as she could.

"My men can be a little too... easily excitable," Vizcarra said. "And, for that, I'm sorry. I hope this will not keep us from working together as partners."

He gestured again, and his men went back to stacking the plants in the road, ultimately a ten-foot pyre worth several hundred thousand dollars.

Vizcarra knew that his diplomatic view of the enterprise was considered a weakness, but those who believed that did not really understand the human heart. If he were feared by the peons, but seen as fair and sparing with his punishments, they would keep their heads down and abide. He would be a curse, like a flood, or a plague of locusts, but something that could be endured. If he were to come into their homes, snapping and frothing like a mad dog, eventually someone would find the courage to put him down like a beast. The twenty-first century really had no room for such beasts.

"We want your cooperation," he said, "your connections, your knowledge of the land and the climate. But, as to your poor excuse for product..."

Vizcarra took a last drag on his cigar and flicked it into the bottom of the pile of gasoline-soaked cannabis. The glowing end touched off the clouds of vapor, which exploded with a sound like a giant rolling out of bed. Flames rose up through the pyre and into a column twenty feet high.

Soon, the fire settled down, as the accelerant was consumed. The bright orange tongues of flame surrendered to clouds of opaque, gray smoke.

Vizcarra's men gathered close around the fire, then they took turns on the down-wind side, where they would breathe deep and dance away to let others take their place. In a matter of a few minutes, his cadre of unkempt mercenaries were reduced to the level of laughing children. Children with AK47s and shotguns.

Abraham did not imbibe, but stood apart from the spontaneous festival to watch the Cunninghams, as their hopes for the future went up in smoke.

SQUIRREL TORTURE PORN

C hris's stomach clenched when he heard the doorbell ring. He didn't know why he should be so nervous, it was only dinner with an old friend. One whom he had thought of frequently over the last twenty years, especially during those dark nights alone, after Amber had deserted them, and Liv retreated into her own little bubble.

No big deal.

He checked himself in the hall mirror, making sure he didn't misbutton his cardigan, or leave his fly open. Then, he opened the door. Olivia stood on the back porch with the setting sun, glowing pink and gold on her blonde hair. She wore a filmy, flowered dress which came halfway down to her knees, the type that always looked in danger of blowing up, or away. She smiled at seeing him, and he felt somehow unworthy of it. Her son was right next to her. Dakota had a tee-shirt, bearing a ferocious cartoon squirrel with the caption: *HIDE YOUR NUTS!*

"Good evening, Mr. Day," the boy said, if nothing else, to make him feel a hundred years old. "Where's Liv?"

"Oh, hey. H-hi guys," he stammered. "Liv's in the kitchen. Go right in."

Dakota slipped passed him.

He gave Olivia a questioning glance, which she responded to with an offhand wave.

Chris felt even more self-conscious.

"You're looking very nice tonight," he said once he summoned up the courage.

"You look nice, too."

"I look like Mr. Rogers."

Olivia chuckled. "Well, he's nice."

"That's not what I was going for."

She stepped forward and leaned in dangerously close.

He froze, not having any idea what the right play for the moment might be.

"I think," she whispered, "you should save the black leather and buckles for the second date."

He looked into her eyes, only inches away, and he was still paralyzed. Part of him was relieved that she hadn't made the move to kiss him. Another part was heartbroken. He felt a strange burning hum behind his eyes, and up his spine, which was driving him toward kissing her, himself.

"If you're going to get back before Dad's bedtime," Liv said quite loudly, "you'd better get going." She had somehow materialized right behind his elbow and caused his heart to skip a beat. Dakota was beside her with a fistful of pretzels and a glass of chocolate milk.

"You sure you're going to be okay here tonight?" Olivia asked him.

"Yeah," he said around a half-chewed pretzel. "Liv's grandma is going to show us some squirrel torture porn."

"It's okay," Liv added. "It's educational."

Olivia made the same micro-expression of horror and concern that Chris made whenever Liv said something, but it passed quickly.

"All right, then," she said before turning to Dakota. "You be good and listen to Mrs. Day."

"Yes, Mom."

Grandma came out of the kitchen to shoo them out. "Don't you two worry about a thing," she growled. "We're going to have fun. You have fun, too."

She grinned at both of them, and Chris remembered what Olivia had said about free advertising on the radio station. He felt a little like an ugly princess being married off for a good alliance.

They each hugged their spawn and slipped out the storm door.

Of course, Chris held the door like a gentleman. As they got down the steps and stopped on sidewalk, it was obvious they were both thinking the exact same thing, *How much damage could the kids actually cause with access to Grandma's guns and tools?*

"Okay if we take your car?" Chris asked. That seemed to be a good, safe topic to start.

"Um, yeah. Sure." Olivia was obviously distracted.

"Look, if you're not up for this, for whatever reason, I'm okay with that. We could just go inside and play *Parcheesi* and watch squirrel torture porn."

"No, I'm good." Olivia shook her head. "It's just been a while. A *long* while. And we're leaving our kids..."

"With a gun-carrying, squirrel-addled sociopath?"

Olivia laughed. "I was so afraid that you hadn't noticed."

"Liv did. She's observant. She told me the first day."

She took his hand, the way they would do as kids, and strolled toward the car.

"They really can't get in any trouble?" she asked, seriously.

"Not as long as they all don't join forces," Chris said. "Then, it could be the end of the world."

* * *

The marijuana pyre took a little over a half an hour to burn down to a smoldering pile of fibrous ash. Vizcarra's men still stuck their heads in the smoke plume to breathe deeply and then stagger back to the trucks. A shouting match broke out the over the last bag of pork rinds.

Vizcarra found the spectacle to be personally embarrassing. He usually expected much more of his men. As much as it bothered him, it mortified the old white couple. The husband fell into a sullen funk, perhaps murderous in his feeble mind, but totally impotent. The wife clung to him and wept as she buried her face in his shabby flannel shirt.

"So," Abraham said cheerily as he bit off the end of his fourth cigar of the evening, "are we ready to talk like adults, or are we going to have to endure even more unpleasantness?"

"Go to hell," John Cunningham muttered.

Vizcarra scowled. "That is not the kind of attitude I'm looking for." He punctuated his statement with a backhand slap to the old man's face.

Soft and weak, Cunningham folded with a spray of blood trickling from the corner of his mouth.

The old woman interposed herself, wrapping herself around her husband and bleating like a wounded goat. Vizcarra found it all a bit dispiriting.

He gestured to his men, who separated the couple and held them still, their knees to the ground, and their throats exposed, like sacrificial lambs.

Vizcarra flipped open his pocket knife. "I understand that you need both hands to be productive farmers," he said. "Both legs, too."

He took three measured steps toward the old woman, the tip of his four-inch blade aimed at her face. "But she doesn't need both eyes, now does she?"

Mrs. Cunningham stared Vizcarra in the eye. Her expression was defiant, hateful, almost triumphant in the fashion of the disgustingly self-righteous.

When Vizcarra flipped a look over toward her husband, he looked frightened, but he wasn't watching what was about to befall his wife. He was looking past her, above her, and into the branches of the trees.

Though suspecting a trick, Vizcarra turned to see what so fascinated the old man. Several of his men had already began staring that way.

There were squirrels in the trees. Dozens of them, perhaps hundreds. They occupied the lowest limbs, sitting cheek by jowl, filling the space with grey fur and bright black eyes.

Vizcarra spun himself around and then did it again.

Squirrels occupied the trees on all sides.

Larger beasts, shaped like squirrels but, three times as large and marked like attack dogs, clung to the trunks and crept downward, slowly.

"What the hell is this?" Vizcarra murmured.

"I don't know," the kneeling woman said with grim humor, "but they look hungry."

They did, Vizcarra realized.

The squirrels leaned forward on their perches, sniffing the air and twitching, as if they were only moments from a leap into space.

"*Vamos, a matarlos y averiguarlo,*" Aguilar shouted as he brought up an AK to his shoulder.

He squeezed off an efficient burst of fire at the nearest black and tan creature. Bullets chewed a line of bark off the tree the beast clung to, at least one round striking it and loosening its grip. It fell, its body making a sound like a bursting melon as it hit the ground.

Only then did Vizcarra have the presence of mind to shout out an order, "¡No *dispares, idiota*! Don't shoot!"

It was already too late for Aguilar. Three of the Rottweiler squirrels flung themselves from the trees and knocked him to the ground. With growls like wildcats, the animals savaged his face and throat, and he slapped them like he was on fire. Smaller squirrels streamed down the tree trunks, or leaped off the lowest branches, to bury the man in a squirming pile of bloody, grey fur. The fur seemed to muffle his screams.

His other men stood, staring at the horrific scene, slack-jawed idiots awaiting his orders.

"NOW you can shoot them!" Vizcarra screamed. He gestured to the men holding the Cunninghams. "Let them go! Kill the fucking squirrels!"

His men opened up. They sprayed their AKs through the upper branches, taking out more leaves and songbirds than squirrels. Some swept their weapons across the path of the rodents, approaching them on the ground, taking out only one rodent in ten. Those who preferred shotguns were best equipped for this attack. Each buckshot round blew away a swathe of squirrels, roughly three foot squared. Unfortunately, the number of squirrels made it like shooting down the ocean. Every hole in the water was instantly filled with more.

Vizcarra threw his switchblade to lodge, point first, into the ground. There was no point in bringing a knife to a squirrel fight. Drawing his Sig .357 from the holster at the small of his back, he pulled the old woman to her feet with his free hand. As he brought her rag doll of a husband to his feet, he told them both, "I believe we should carry on our business discussions somewhere more comfortable."

He slow walked them, through the massacre, toward his white Escalade. His men fell around them, one by one. Vizcarra assessed that the animals' actions were motivated by both vengeance and hunger. His men who had shot first were being eaten first. The rodents flowed, like water, and covered grown men, like carpets, as they gnawed them down into twitching mounds of bone and viscera.

Vizcarra pulled the Cunninghams up short as he got close enough to see a herd of squirrels taking the high ground atop his Cadillac. Their fur was drenched in blood, and their heads and tails twitched as if they were on meth. He could see only one way to get inside without being attacked. He waved to two of his men, their names he couldn't recall, but they wouldn't need them much longer.

"Get those squirrels off the top of my car," he shouted. "We can all lock ourselves inside once they're gone!"

His men didn't need much encouragement to shoot things. Several rounds swept the animals off the roof. Stray shots chipped the paint and spalled the bullet-proof glass.

Vizcarra let loose a few choice words but, if that was the cost of survival, so be it.

He dragged Mrs. Cunningham along by one hand and rushed for the car before another wave of squirrels arrived. He hoped that she still had her husband in tow but, again, that was not his highest priority. He punched out the code on the door and pitched her into the SUV.

Mr. Cunningham had fallen behind. The squirrels fell from

the trees upon him with small sharp claws and bright biting teeth. The two men with guns behind him were already pushed to the ground by the weight of small, hungry animals. That didn't keep them from squeezing off shots, even though they were already dead men. One round struck the glass beside Vizcarra. He forced the old woman into the passenger seat so he could slip in behind the wheel and lock the door.

The old man slapped his bloody hands on the driver's side window, leaving red smears on the glass. His head was a crown of angry squirrels.

Vizcarra thought to spare one slug to put him out of his misery, but there was no way to open the door, or the window, without inviting in the squirrels. Also, the shrieking woman at his back might not understand the gesture.

Instead, he hit the start button and gunned the Cadillac's engine. Though the windshield was covered in blood and fur, he could see a hellish scene around the clearing, as friends and comrades were being gnawed to the bone. He took off toward the road, even though the wipers and washer spray only turned his view into a carnal watercolor. He held to the road, with difficulty, as he ran over mounds of bodies and vermin.

MOTHER OF SQUIRRELS

The Sciuriologist knew Sluggo and his cousin, Bubba, left a lot to be desired as minions. She had seen evidence of that over and over again, but their refusal to betray confidences trumped any lack of mental acuity, or physical skill. The two had been able to pilfer fifty-seven bales of marijuana from different local farmers and bring them all to the silo.

There had been some grumbling during transporting the product to the bottom of the one-hundred and-fifty-foot silo. As a positive behavioral modifier, she left two twenty-four packs of Coors near the burn site, like a piece of cheese in the center of a maze. As she watched, Sluggo and Bubba laid out the bundles in the proscribed ring patterns on the lowermost catwalk. Occasionally, they would teeter on the edge of the retainer grid and risked a fall down into the cesspit full of squirrel droppings, urine, and leftovers of a million carnivore meals. Her minions had already broken open the beer.

As those two wobbled and grumbled, the Sciuriologist ran

through the video displays of each of her breeding colonies set up along the walls of the silo in a virtual bed check. She had bred several races of squirrels during her last two decades of research. Sapper Squirrels were tough, and fast at tunneling through anything, including reinforced concrete. Blackout Squirrels had an innate craving for plastic wiring insulation and an incredible resistance to electrocution. The Judas Squirrels proved to be intelligent and courageous in their hard-wired role of luring larger predators into ambush.

The jewel of her genetic engineering crown were the Avenger Squirrels, an ill-tempered and carnivorous mixture of *Ratufa indica*, the Indian giant squirrel, the honey badger, and the Staffordshire Bull Terrier. A single one of those, weighing in at fifteen kilograms, could handily take down a grown man if it had the element of surprise on its side.

Sluggo and Bubba often looked over their shoulders, as if not entirely trusting the Sciuriologist, or her babies. The men snatched up the remaining beer once they had finished the marijuana array and dashed for the access hatch. She had thought about sealing them in as an *hors d'oeuvre* for her babies, but opted to stick with her original plan in dealing with them. It certainly wouldn't matter if they talked to the authorities once they got off the compound.

Her revenge would be final and, most likely, the end of a long and bitter life. She never expected to outlive those in Crickson who had injured her so many years ago.

As her two lackeys rode the elevator up to the surface, the Sciuriologist sealed the silo, triggered the igniters, and slowed the ventilation fans. Quickly, the entire structure filled with fumes that would give all of her progeny a major buzz. They would be happy little rodents for the space of an hour. Then, the internal cannabinoid pathways in their brains would overload, and they would feel an overwhelming need to feed. She would roll back the concrete blast door at the mouth of the silo and unleash her creations upon a sleeping town. It would be the most horrible and beautiful thing she could imagine.

* * *

Great-Grandma Iris laid back on her crappy green couch, sound asleep. Her head was tilted over the back, and her mouth hung wide open. She made a gargling, choking noise as she exhaled. Her false teeth, hanging by a thread of pink adhesive, flapped backwards and forwards in time with the noise.

"You know," Liv said, "this is just a little bit more disturbing than the squirrel torture films."

"More fun to watch," Dakota agreed.

Liv wiggled from under her spot at the coffee table and stood, dusting off bits of string cheese and squirrel jerky.

"Well, she's going to be out for the night," she said. "You want to go somewhere fun?"

"We can't just leave. Won't she wake up and notice we're gone?"

"Nah, she's a real deep sleeper. When she's out like this, she doesn't even respond to thumbtacks, or hot needles."

Dakota looked a little sick, as he had time to work over her admission in his mind.

Liv just shook her head as she headed toward the door. "Come on, her golf cart is charged up out back."

"Hold on a second," Dakota said.

"What's wrong, you scared?" Liv gestured at the spectacle on the couch. "You wanna watch that all night?"

"No," he said as he pulled a burner phone from his pocket. "I just wanted to invite Cesar. That's okay, isn't it?"

"Yeah," Liv chuckled. "Go ahead and call him."

"Oh, I don't call him. I send him a fake telemarketing text. The product it's pitching is the code word for where we'll meet." Dakota looked up from his texting with an earnest expression. "His uncle really doesn't like him hanging out with me."

"I don't see why," Liv replied. "You're just teaching him how to think like a drug dealer."

REUNION

C hris found himself in the local Applebee's, sitting across the table from table from Olivia. It was ridiculous to try to pick up things from when they were twelve, but he was sweating and afraid, anyway. Terrified if he might say something wrong, Chris was even more scared that he might say something right. His mind couldn't visualize a stopping point in the chain of events between a passionate kiss goodnight and a no holds barred legal battle for custody and alimony.

"So," he said in hopes of avoiding disaster, "why didn't you ever leave Crickson?"

Olivia took a sip of her Long Island iced tea before answering.

"Well, I did, actually. When I was nineteen, I took up with this guy named Duryea, and we ran down to Las Vegas to get married. We stayed there for a while. He hosted high stakes poker games, and I would serve drinks, stark naked, to... keep the other players... distracted."

She took another sip of her drink and shrugged, calmly, like she was telling him about Dakota's last soccer game.

"There were a few times, quite a few times, when he'd put my ass on the poker table to cover bets when he ran out of money. I'd do whatever the winner wanted, and Duryea got a chance to recoup his losses. I'm pretty sure that one of those guys is Dakota's biological father. There were a couple of pretty ones with blonde hair."

Though he hadn't expected her to stay a virgin, really, he felt enormous pressure trying to compete with her history. From just what she'd said tonight, Olivia had slept with more women than he did. Chris really regretted that he had made himself the designated driver for tonight.

"So, anyways," she continued, "when it finally all fell apart, I came back here and, with the settlement from my ex, I was able to get the loan for the radio station. Since then, I've decided to not date anyone who isn't up for a sainthood, or has a penis. Nothing personal."

The ginger ale really wasn't doing the trick for Chris. He needed vodka.

"Anyway, when we started broadcasting, the local pot farmers were getting hammered by the Feds, and that was the only way some families were making money after the dairy market collapsed. We started reporting the cops' movements, gave them a fighting chance, and got a ton of listeners."

"So that's why Rafael has such problems with you."

Olivia raised her eyebrows and squelched her mouth to one side at the mention of their old friend.

"Well, that gets a bit awkward," she said. "You've got to promise me you'll never breathe a word of this."

"He nearly shot me over a remark about pubic hair. Don't worry."

Olivia fixed him with a long doubtful gaze, sipped her drink, and went on.

"We had a long talk just before I left to wreck my life with my ex. An all-nighter."

"Drunk?" Chris asked.

"Of course," she said. "You remember how he would always get grumpy when I gave you a hug, or a kiss, on the cheek?"

"Yeah. There were some of the times when I thought he'd clock me."

"So I asked him why, if he was so jealous, didn't he ever make a move on me after you didn't come back?"

"And?"

"He told me he was never jealous of you; he was actually jealous of me."

Chris sat there for several long moments, parsing that sentence, and then tried to match it to everything he remembered. The effort must have shown on his face.

"Yes, he's batting for the other team," she stated. "Taking a knee on the field, whatever sports metaphor you like."

"And he was in love with me?"

Olivia nodded, then drank.

"But, he's so..."

"Macho?" she suggested. "In Vegas, there's just as many gay bouncers and Marines as hair dressers. Taunt them at your own risk."

"Wow..."

"You're not going to freak out, or anything, are you?"

Chris propped his head on the fingertips of one hand, letting it lean off to one side, just as his whole worldview was doing.

"Nawww. Why would I do that?"

Olivia bobbled her head, going both "yes" and "no" at the

same time as she looked anywhere in the restaurant but directly at him.

"So," she said, "do you think the kids are all right with your grandma?"

* * *

After they'd picked up Cesar in the golf cart, he and Dakota chattered away like they hadn't seen each other for weeks. The steady stream of nerdisms made her head hurt as she concentrated on keeping the cart on the road. She had a quick moment of panic when she spotted the pin-points of colored light in the rearview mirror. Then, there was a moment of relief when she realized the boys would quit talking.

"Quick," Cesar shouted from the back deck of the golf cart, "turn off down here!"

Liv saw that there was a dirt track to her right, two sets of ruts in the grass that probably led to a fishing hole at the river below. She cranked the wheel and aimed the cart for the grass in the center. It rolled downhill a bit and across the ruts, jostling Cesar off of the back.

Dakota dowsed the headlights just as the red and blue lights of the Sheriff's SUV colored the leaves of the trees around them.

"Scatter!" Dakota stage whispered.

Liv and he went out opposite sides and huddled close to the ground.

"You think your uncle is after you?" Liv asked Cesar.

"You can never tell."

A green and white four-wheel drive roared past them on the road, its red and blue lights illuminating the trees and bushes around the cart. It was gone in just a second. The three kids rose back to their feet as the lights and sound receded into the distance.

"So," Dakota asked Liv, "you still want to go to the video store?"

"Sure." Liv got behind the wheel of the golf cart. "Just as long as the video doesn't have any narration, education, or redeeming social value."

"We're not going to sit through any girly films, like *My Little Pony*, or *The Princess and the Frog*.

"Uh-uh." Dakota perched on the back deck as Cesar took shotgun.

"Hell, no!" Liv said as she backed the cart onto the country road. "I was hoping the remake of *I Spit on Your Grave* was out by now."

For whatever reason, the boys didn't say another word for the rest of the drive.

LET SLIP THE SQUIRRELS OF WAR

The Sciuriologist's two idiot minions loitered beside the ten-ton steel blast door on the surface. She was able to see them both clearly through the night vision cameras mounted on the sentry guns. They sat on the bumper of the dual rear-tired pick-up, drank beer, and occasionally dodged the swinging tails of the cattle in the bed. After only a half hour, the case of beer was nearly depleted.

"I hope," she announced over the PA system, "That one of you two is still fit to drive."

"Don't worry about us," Bubba called out, "we can hold our alcohol."

Sluggo belched loudly, perhaps as an expansion of Bubba's remarks. He removed his seed company cap and crushed his empty beer can on his forehead.

"I am over-flowing with confidence," the Sciuriologist muttered. "Stand clear, I am opening the blast door."

She shook her head as she threw the switches that engaged the heavy-duty electric motors. A little chemical reinforcement seemed only reasonable for what she was asking of her hench-men, but too much liquid courage was sure to lead to solid stupidity.

The hatch slowly slid open with the speed and sound of a glacier. She could feel vibrations of steel against concrete in her bones and gut, like fingernails on chalkboard. All the sensors before her indicated the squirrels had the same reaction, in spite of the cannabis. In the terms of the modern culture, it was "harshing their mellow."

The Sciuriologist smiled. That was exactly what she had hoped for.

The surface cameras showed a slit of about four feet opened as the blast door drew back. A thin column of smoke rose up from the silo, which dissipated in the light breeze.

Bubba wobbled up to the silo's edge. At first, the scientist thought he was placing his head in the smoke column to get a lungful of THC. Then, he leaned back his head and hawked up a mass of mucous and saliva to spit down into the pit at his feet. He shook his head, obviously unable to hear the impact over the grinding of the door and ventilation fans below.

Stats of the rodents in the upper reaches of the complex started to spike, excited by the smell of food and the sight of the sky.

"You had better step away from there," the Sciuriologist warned.

"I'm not going to fall in," Bubba muttered.

"I'm not concerned about that, but my babies can smell the meat on your bones."

She could see the two rednecks look anxiously from one to the other.

"I need you to lead them away from the bunker here to the heart of Crickson. There is a maroon Honda Odyssey in the

Lucky's parking lot. The remainder of your payment is in the pocket behind the driver's seat."

One of the cattle inside the stock rack in the pickup lowed plaintively.

"Your squirrels are going to track the smell of hamburger on the hoof?" Sluggo asked.

"Not quite," she said. "Please don't make any sudden moves."

"What the fuck?" muttered Bubba.

She keyed in the infrared targeting of the sentinel guns, set the maximum size parameter over five-hundred kilos while adding two no-kill signals for her minions, and initiated. A brief burst of fifty caliber fire chewed through the cattle and most of the bed structure of the truck. Blood, and other fluids, began to trickle down to the ground below.

"Any questions?" she asked brightly.

"Fuck no," one of her two associates mumbled.

"Good," she said, "you should be leaving now. My Avenger Squirrels can reach speeds of up to twenty-five miles an hour over short distances."

Sluggo slipped his cap back on his head and dashed for the driver's door. His cousin was a few seconds behind him on the other side.

"The keys for the Honda are in the glove box there," the Sciuriologist said. "Drive carefully."

The bullet-riddled pickup sped toward the gateway, leaving a trail of blood behind it.

* * *

Vizcarra was having real problems keeping the Cadillac on the road. The windshield was still a reddish smear, even after three washings. There was something red and meaty caught under the passenger side wiper which left another track of blood every time it moved. The sun had set, and not even the high beams could cut through the combined darkness and gore. Oh, and the Cunningham woman still wouldn't stop screaming.

He needed both hands to avoid running off into the deep ditches, on either side, or he would have slapped her. Instead, he hunched down over the steering wheel to peer through the one persistent clear spot and stepped on the gas.

"Could you please stop that?" he shouted. "It is very distracting!"

He dared a glance over to see her curled up on the floor beneath the dashboard and glove box.

"You can't sit there," he said. "It's dangerous."

Perhaps she had a lower threshold of fear after being kidnapped by armed men and seeing those men, and her husband, being eaten by squirrels. Still, that kind of behavior bred nasty accidents.

He returned his eyes to the road in time to catch the oncoming police SUV appear around the curve in full lights and sirens mode. Somehow, they were both in the same lane. The ram's head logo on the grill seemed to be aimed right at his forehead, like a guided missile. Then, his world was enveloped in light and noise. Vizcarra was hit really, really hard in the face with a big, white balloon.

* * *

Sgt. Chuck had been on his way to a "shots fired" call on the federal lands when he crashed. He had taken just a second to look down at his laptop to coordinate backup. When he looked up, the white Cadi was looming up in his headlights. He had just a second to realize that the oncoming vehicle was covered with blood, and fur, before they collided, and Newton's Laws of Motion took to seriously kicking his ass.

As the cab of his truck filled with white powder, and his ears rang, Chuck fumbled around for the rescue hammer which he kept in the central console. He punched and twisted the spike end through the plastic fabric of the airbag and pressed it down out of his way.

The first thing he could see through the steam and the smoke was that the two airbags were still inflated in the other vehicle. Most likely, the driver and the passenger had been knocked unconscious, something he was hoping to do himself.

He snatched up the handset from the dashboard and clicked to clear the channel.

"Ten thirty-three, ten thirty-three. Head-on collision with civilian vehicle on Day Farm Road, just east of Lutman. Over"

The dispatcher clicked back in an instant. "Honey, are you okay?'

"I am intact," Sgt. Chuck said with a sigh. "Best send over a hook and an ambulance to my location."

"People in the other vehicle injured?"

"Give me time." Sgt. Chuck realized he was on an open and recorded line. "I mean, give me a second to check them out. Over and out."

He pitched the mic onto the other seat and opened his door. The front end had been pushed back enough on his side to wedge against the door. It squealed and complained as he pushed, but he was able to pry his way clear. He laid one hand on the pommel of his baton as he approached the passenger door of the Cadi.

"Is everyone all right in there?" he called out, loud and clear.

There was a flurry of motion in the front seats. It looked like people were beating the airbags out of their way, though it was hard to tell. Chuck had seen the mess a deer hit could make of a car with blood, hair, and offal. This was way worse, like the SUV had been run through a car wash run with liquefied venison.

"If you can hear me," he shouted, "I need for you to come out, real nice and slow, with your hands where I can see them."

The nearest door flew open and, someone came screeching out. "Ohmigod, Sergeant Chuck! They ate John!"

He was already on his way to draw his sidearm when he recognized the swirl of bloodied grey hair and blue flannel.

"Mrs. Cunningham!" Like half his generation in Crickson, she had fed him raw milk and oatmeal raisin cookies as a kid. "What the hell happened here?"

She wrapped her arms around his waist and wept in his chest. Between sobs, she gave him a story that sounded something like this, "The Mexicans, they kidnapped us, and they stole all our weed and burned it. And, just when their boss was about to cut out my eye, the killer squirrels fell out of the trees and started to eat the Mexicans, and they looked like Dobermans and chewed up the men with guns, but it was the little grey ones that ate John's head, and then we jumped into this car and ran away!"

But that couldn't be right.

As he tried to work out what she *really* said and patted her bloody head, he realized that he should really be wearing exam gloves for the amount of bodily fluids around. Then, he looked a little more carefully at the open door behind her. There were several pale circles on the tinted window, spalling from small arms fire where it struck bullet-resistant glass. Missing paint on the body indicated impacts from double-ought buckshot.

This wasn't just a bizarre animal-hit accident. This was a rolling crime scene.

Chuck shuffled backwards toward his truck, with Mrs. Cunningham securely wrapped around his midsection. He used one hand to pop open the back door as he peeled himself free of the sobbing woman. He nudged her toward the seat and tried to be soothing.

"Here, Mrs. C," he murmured. "You have a seat right here while I check everything else out. Okay?"

She complied with a shaky nod and a sniffle. He patted her gently on the knee once she had settled.

"Now, your friend over there in the Cadillac, he doesn't have any guns, or anything, does he?"

Her mind seemed to clear just long enough to look up at him as if he were a total fucking moron.

"Of course, he does," she said, "he's the Mexican the squirrels didn't eat."

"Uh-huh."

He keyed the radio mic which hung from his shoulder once he was a pace or two away from her.

"Hello, dispatch, I'm going to be needing backup. Over."

He thought over his situation and made a quick amendment to his request. "All of it, please."

The voice coming back over the airwaves sounded harried. "What is your situation?"

Sgt. Chuck knew that he could spend the rest of the evening talking about his situation, but it would be best to just hit the highlights:

"I have a bulletproof Cadi covered in blood, and fur, that came from the direction of my shots fired call. I have a sweet little old lady who, only now, stopped screaming." He wiped away the sweat accumulating on his brow with the back of his mic hand as he rested the other hand on top of his holstered weapon. "I have a diminishing chance of living long enough to collect my pension. I could use a little help."

There was a second of dead air, and then dispatch was back on the line.

"We are stretched paper thin tonight. A ton of accidents, missing persons, animal incidents. I've got three separate reports of people being attacked by killer squirrels. It's a mad house out there."

Chuck shot a glance back at the old woman curled up in a ball on his back seat.

"Killer... squirrels... did you say?"

"Why, do you have some there?"

"I've had a report." Chuck gently pushed the back door shut, locking in Mrs. Cunningham safely. "Get somebody out here as soon as you can, huh? Over and out."

He moved up to the front end of the Cadi and stopped. He could still see through the windshield while being close enough to the open door to be heard.

"Sir, I'm going to need you to step out of the car now."

"No, thank you," the driver called out deferentially. "I'm quite comfortable where I am."

Chuck sniffed and popped the flashlight from his belt. He shined the light through the bloody glass with his left, like they did in the academy. A dark-skinned man in a bloodied white suit stared back.

The driver dropped below the dashboard and out of sight. Chuck took one step to the left, and two to the back. He drew and braced his gun hand on the other as he did.

"Get out of that car now, sir! I need to see your hands!"

The man did not comply, but he didn't come out with guns blazing, either. He pulled the door shut and then engaged all the locks.

Chuck stood in middle of the road, trying to calculate the next reasonable move. The good news was that the bad actor had sealed himself inside a bulletproof can. He wasn't going to be able to shoot out any more than Chuck could shoot in. The bad news just came trickling in.

A black pickup truck came around the curve at high speed and just barely under control. It pulled hard to the left and went off the blacktop a few feet to avoid hitting Chuck and the two disabled cars. As it pulled back onto the road, the bump bounced the dead cows in the back, high enough into the air that Chuck could see. Even though he had thrown himself back against the wrecked Cadi, he also noticed the bullet holes in the side.

Just that fast, the truck was gone, heading toward Lutman, and probably into town. Chuck could hear faint noises in the distance once it was gone. Barks, squeals, and chattering; it sounded like what he would imagine a few thousand killer squirrels might sound like. He jumped into his SUV and put in another radio call.

"Um, hello, dispatch. I've got another request for this location. Could you send out Animal Control and see if Derrell Walters still has those Army surplus flamethrowers he used for clearing brush? I'd appreciate it. Over and out."

He pulled his door to shut, but his pushing to open it had bent it out of true. No matter how much weight he put into it, he couldn't force it to latch. Preparing for a last stand, he unlocked the shotgun between the front seats and placed his sig on the dashboard, for easy reach. As he held the door as close to shut as possible, he hoped all of this was just hysteria.

JOY RIDE

"Here, snipe! Here, snipe," Bob Zimmerman called out into the darkness as he held open the feed bag in front of him. His friends in marching band insisted that they all had gone on snipe hunts before their first shows. Gene, John, and Luke had dropped him off at the woods near Dicob's farm just after sunset. That was the time of highest snipe activity, they told him.

So, here he was, out standing in a field, left holding the bag. The night kept getting colder, and darker, just as his thoughts about his band mates were also getting colder and darker.

"Here, snipe," he called out, not as much to attract the little birds, as to prove to his buddies that he was still going along with the game. He was sure they were lurking in the bushes, drinking beer, and stifling their laughter. As the night wore on, he imagined all sorts of awful things he could stuff in their mouths to keep them quiet.

At about the three-hour mark, there was a commotion in the bushes. The leaves thrashed from side to side, and animals

SQUIRREL APOCALYPSE • 113

squealed and barked and chattered. It sounded like all the woodland creatures were murdering each other gangland style.

"Here... snipe?"

Bob had never bothered to ask if snipes were dangerous. From the noises they made, they were armed with mallets and chainsaws.

A more human set of screams broke out, and three boys leaped out of the undergrowth. Gene, John, and Luke, those bastards, had been hiding no more than twenty feet away. He was no longer angry with them after he saw why they were screaming. He just felt a wave of nausea and panic.

Little animals swarmed all over their bodies, clawing and biting at any soft spots they could find. Blood streamed down his friends' faces as they beat at the furry little monsters. It took only seconds for his friends to drop to the ground, kicking and weeping. Then the animals came for him.

Bob's last thought before he was overrun by the little creatures was, *Gee, snipes look an awful lot like squirrels.*

* * *

As first dates went, Chris thought he'd had more pleasant root canals. Still, he smiled as he held open the door for her to leave the restaurant. He had imagined a reunion with Olivia for over a decade now, probably starting shortly after Liv was born and Amber stopped sleeping with him. It had been pure idiocy to believe she had been waiting around for him to pick up their relationship where he had left it at puppy love. Maybe that's why tonight's dinner felt like it went on in dog years.

"So," he said with cheerful lilt in his voice, "what do you think the kids are doing right now?"

Olivia chuckled, but then winced at his question.

"Probably the same thing they were doing when we started dinner, but with a lot less energy."

"Oh yeah, that..." Two hours of Grandma Day's favorite videos could kill any spirit.

He looked any way but toward her as they crossed the parking lot to her car. That's why he caught sight of the golf cart on a side street. It was green, with a white canvass top, just like Grandma's. A blonde girl was driving, with an even blonder boy in the back. Someone with dark hair and skin sat in the seat beside her. They were too far away to see clearly, but Chris knew almost immediately.

He went from the depths of suicidal depression over his love life to absolutely flummoxed in less time than it took to say the phrase. Then, he got pissed.

"Or, maybe," he snarled, "they stole Grandma's golf cart and drove the seven miles to town to drop by the video store and pick up something they liked."

Olivia looked at him as if he were insane. "Why would you say something ridiculous like that?"

Chris started running for the car before he answered, "Because I just saw those sneaky little bastards about two blocks over. Quick, we need to get after them."

Olivia took a second to process all of that. Then, that look of parental homicide flashed through her eyes and she clip-clopped on her chunky heels to the driver's door. It took her a second to work the locks. Then, they were both in the vehicles, and she had the motor running.

"What the hell were they thinking?" she said.

"I don't know. Maybe they were driven insane by squirrel porn."

"Squirrel torture porn," she corrected. "It's even worse."

She made a noise of frustration as she overpowered the turn

SQUIRREL APOCALYPSE • 115

out of the parking lot and barely missed a pickup at the meters. Chris held on to the dashboard and scanned the streets ahead. The taillights and traffic lights made it hard to see, but he thought he spotted a familiar green blob.

"That looks like them, about three blocks ahead. I think they're turning left."

"Well, that's the only place my son will be going for the next month."

"Just a month? I'm grounding Liv until after she graduates college."

Olivia made the left turn after the golf cart. It felt like there were only two wheels on the road.

"Sometime, we're going to have to talk about why you named your daughter after me."

Chris felt a rush of ice-cold terror in his gut as a counter-point to the fear for his life he got from her driving. He stammered out a response as quickly as the words would form. "It's not what you think. Amber's great-aunt was named Olivia."

"Uh-huh," she muttered. "Hold on to that thought."

She made a right turn immediately after the left and then pulled into the lot of the Quikee Fill convenience store. They pulled enough reverse gees on the stop to pull Chris's seat belt into a painful lockdown across his shoulder.

Olivia blocked in the golf cart in its spot in front of the store. The kids were already on the sidewalk and staring back at them. Dakota looked like he was staring down a firing squad. Liv was sullen and unrepentant. Cesar, upon seeing the parents, raised his hands and then interlaced his fingers behind his head. His uncle had taught him the drill, it seemed.

Olivia was already out of the car before Chris could unbuckle.

"What the hell did you think you were doing?"

Dakota chuckled and tried to charm his way out of his ugly situation. "Mom, Mr. Day, I didn't think you would be done with dinner so soon."

"Definitely," Olivia responded. "That's why you thought you wouldn't get caught. What made you think that joyriding on a golf cart in the middle of the night was a bright idea?"

"We just wanted to come into town and rent a movie," Liv replied. "It's no big deal."

"This little go-cart is not street legal," Olivia said. "You want to guess what would have happened if you got rear-ended by some drunk in a pickup truck?"

Chris finally got to join in the interrogation.

"Did Grandma say this was all right?" he asked Liv. When she wouldn't answer, he grew worried. "You didn't kill Grandma, did you?"

Liv sniffed, her primary form of communication with him. "No, we didn't kill Grandma. She passed out on her own."

Chris saw a look pass between Dakota and Cesar and, for a moment, he wondered how close to home his joke about homicide really was.

Olivia threw her arms up in the air in frustration. "All right, that's it! Everybody in the car. We'll sort this out when we get home."

"What about the golf cart," Dakota asked. "Aren't you afraid it might get stolen?"

Cesar covered his face with one hand and turned away.

Liv just looked at her friend with the same contempt she usually showed her father.

"It's been stolen once already." Olivia snatched the keys out of the ignition and gestured sharply. "Not another word. Just get in the car."

Chris held open the back door on his side and let the kids

file in, one by one. After he shut them in, he slid in on the shotgun position. Though he had done nothing wrong, he was afraid to look Olivia in the eye, himself.

She fumed in the driver's seat for a few moments, her hands on the wheel, her elbows locked tight. She then closed her eyes. She took in a long breath and released it and, in letting it go, she erased at least the surface appearance of her upset. Olivia started the car and put it in reverse.

She had to slam on the brakes suddenly, as a black pickup sped down the street right behind her. It was gone and turning toward the big shopping center before Chris even knew it was there.

"Fucking assholes," she hissed. "That is why I was so upset about you being on the road."

Most of the others in the car nodded and agreed, but silently.

"Ms. Halverson," Cesar chimed up. "There must be something going on. That black pickup truck was full of bullet holes."

"That is none of our concern right now," Olivia responded in a calm parental tone. "And another fantastical story isn't going to distract us from what you three have done wrong."

"But—"

"No more talking." Olivia turned on the radio, with enough volume to drown out any further conversation. Her radio station was playing eighties oldies tonight. "I think I'd like to listen to some music now."

Chris looked out the window as Olivia got the car on the pavement. The local Radio Shack was right next door to the Quikee Fill. He'd rather look at the window posters for radio-control toys than risk getting in the middle of any more conversations.

The Fine Young Cannibals were interrupted by the Voice.

She sounded worried, but still evoked the soundtrack of a foreign porn film.

"This is an emergency announcement. The Humboldt County Sheriff's Department is asking everyone to please stay in their homes, or take shelter immediately. Numerous reports of animal attacks are coming in on the north side of the county. Some think it is a population of rabid squirrels, but there are no established facts yet. Everybody, please remain calm and report any unusual incidents to the sheriff's department, or the state police, through nine-one-one. We now return you to our regularly scheduled program."

Olivia drove on in silence. The kids were cowed for a moment, themselves.

Chris was the first to say anything. "My God," he sighed, "she made even that sound sexy."

"We've got to get home right away," Liv said. "If Grandma hears about this, she's going to lose her mind."

"That's exactly what I was thinking," Olivia said as she floored the gas. In a minute or two, they were on the country road which led to her farm.

Chris had slipped into a hyperaware state with the trouble they'd had already, and the promise of Grandma waging World War Squirrel. He saw the flash of white fur and reflections of little eyes long before Olivia had.

"Slow down," he said, "there's something in the middle of the road."

"Wonderful."

She pumped the brakes and brought the SUV to under twenty miles an hour. About fifty feet away, Chris could make out what was happening. A deer rose up on its hind legs on the yellow center line. Little grey and red animals scaled the deer's legs and hung from his haunches. The deer brought his head down and swept the ground with his antlers. Squirrels flew left and right, their pale bellies and fluffy tails giving them away.

Olivia let the car coast slowly toward the scrum. No one in the car could come up with anything useful to say.

More squirrels, dozens of them, scampered from the tall grass on either side of the road to join in the fight. The stag went down and was covered with ravenous rodents. While most piled on to the twitching corpse, a few turned toward their car. They bared bloody teeth and flicked their tails franticly.

"No way in fucking hell this is happening," she said through gritted teeth. "Don't look, kids!"

She stepped on the gas and drove through the herd of rodents like a momma grizzly bear behind the wheel.

One or two squirrels leaped up onto the hood, but slid back and away as the car hit fifty.

"We'd better get to Grandma's right away," Chris said.

"You think?" Olivia said as she focused on the road ten feet beyond her high-beams.

EXTREME PEST CONTROL

In spite of the chaos outside her home, Irene Day felt strangely calm, as if this was the moment she had been preparing for her whole life. At first, she was terrified and then furious when she realized that the children had slipped out and taken her golf cart with them. Then, she realized that she had been awakened by the sound of squirrels. Not just the barks and squawks of a single, irritable squirrel, not the staccato tapping of claws on her slate roof. This was a torrent of sound coming from a deluge of squirrels.

She moved as quickly as she could with her bad knees, setting out weapons at each ground floor window, according to her ultimate battle plan. In the time it took to put everything in place, she saw squirrels of all description surround her home, like unwashed hippies at Woodstock. She had only minutes before the little bastards started chewing through the external wires and wooden clapboards to get at her.

She sprinted to the bookcase next to the fireplace and pulled out *The Anarchist's Cookbook*, Sun's *Art of War*, and a fistful of military bulletins about asymmetric warfare. At the back of that space, Iris kept a big red button under a protective acrylic cover. She laughed maniacally as she unlocked the lid and exposed the trigger.

"You little bastards picked on the wrong old lady," she said as she hit the big red button.

Thirty-six improvised M5 MCCMs, the non-lethal variation on the Claymore developed by the US government to pacify Iraqi prison riots, detonated all at once. Each device she had built right there on her dining room table: a Styrofoam meat tray, roughly eight inches by six inches, lined with Airsoft plastic pellets and then filled with homebrew plastic explosives and set to detonate with an electric match, like kids used for model rockets. With a pinch of cayenne to repel the rodents that survived and a metal plate to direct the blast away from her home, each was a pretty effective device.

M5s were non-lethal, but only for something with the mass of an adult human. The high-speed plastic shot would tear a dozen new assholes in something the size of a squirrel.

It would also be pretty damn debilitating for anything the size of a woodchuck.

Probably wouldn't do much good for her landscaping, either.

All three dozen mines made a deafening sound, which she hadn't prepared for. Her ears rang as the smoke and dust settled. It took her a few seconds to notice that the clouds of debris were both inside, and outside, the house. The compression wave from the blast had shattered every window in the house, while knocking down every picture and tchotchke hanging on the walls.

She shook her head, picked up her favorite shotgun, the twelve-gauge Mossberg security special with the front pistol grip, and stumbled toward her back door. Her impeccably neat home was now an obstacle course of debris. The mud room was strewn with broken mason jars and pickled vegetables, where the canned goods shelves gave way. She swore at all the canning she would have to redo because of the damned squirrels, one more reason to blow the fur off their little rat tails with the birdshot she had loaded in the shotgun.

She kicked open her back door with her safety off and a shell in the chamber. She wasn't taking any chances on the little rodents mounting a counter attack.

There weren't any of them intact enough to attack. Not much of anything was. All of her shrubs surrounding the house were blown away with only a few scorched-looking twigs still rooted in the earth. All of the surviving foliage pointed directly away from the house in all directions. Her assortment of bird-feeders and whirligigs got themselves blown into matchwood out to a distance of thirty or forty feet. Their remains piled up on the far side of the gravel driveway, along with mats of grey fur and bits of squirrel meat. Her pickup had piles of that debris deposited around the two tires nearest the house, like snow drifts. Its paint was blasted off down to the bare metal all along that side.

The bark and smaller branches on the cedar in her backyard had been removed, instantaneously, by the anti-squirrel charge. The naked wood looked like it had been polished. The magnolia in her front yard looked the same. There were also a few rectangular holes in her house's siding, where her devices pushed themselves inward as they shot out the pellets the other way. Maybe she had used just a little too much explosives. But there weren't any squirrels left to bother her.

She wheeled around with her shotgun on her hip as the weakened front porch roof collapsed with a sound like a second explosion.

* * *

Rafael was first on the scene for the officer needs assistance call. He couldn't make sense of the mess as he first came around the corner, it just was a large mass, illuminated with flashing lights. The single object resolved itself into a white SUV and Sgt. Chuck's patrol truck mashed nose to nose, probably at high speed. Smoke and steam still escaped from beneath their hoods. There was no sign of life, though.

He parked his truck across the road from Chuck's and checked in with dispatch. The exchange was only a few words and grunts, enough to tell base he was still alive and to inform Rafael that things were too insane for him to expect any backup. He slipped out of the SUV carefully, flashlight in hand, watchful for oncoming traffic, either way, or bad actors hiding on the other side of the wreck. Nothing that simple presented itself at the scene.

First off, there was a carpet of dead animals laid out around the half-open driver's door of the SUV. Those that weren't torn in pieces by shotgun fire looked like squirrels, mostly. There were a few larger corpses with black and tan fur and a set of teeth like a wolf. The rest looked like exposed muscle, bones and entrails.

"Remember the Alamo," Rafael murmured to himself.

As he drew closer, he noticed a bloody combat boot on the ground. The foot seemed to still be in it. Rafael felt a wave of emotion rush over him then, a chaotic mix he didn't have time to analyze. He could tell, though, that fear and disgust were easily outweighed by the visceral desire to beat something with a stick. He pulled his baton from the ring on his Sam Browne belt and used it to open the door.

The sight hit Rafael like a gut punch. Sgt. Chuck had been a big man in life. What was left of him, slumped across the front seat, still looked big with most of the flesh chewed from his bones. He had gone down fighting, too. His shotgun laid on the floor beside several expended plastic shells and brass from his sidearm. His Sig Sauer laid in the bloody mess where his lap should have been.

"Oh, Christ, Chuck," Rafael moaned. "What the hell could have done this to you?"

Something moved in the periphery of his vision and he swiveled quickly to pin down whatever it was with his light. A squirrel, its belly gorged to the size of a tennis ball, was wedged in the black metal grill between front and back seat. As hard as it would thrash and wriggle, it couldn't force its way through. It barked and snarled at Rafael, but remained stuck.

Swearing profusely in three languages, Rafael struck it in the head with his stick until it stopped moving. The sound of scurrying and gnawing still came from the backseat. More engorged killer squirrels. From the white hair on the seat and scraps of the familiar plaid flannel shirt, he guessed it was Mrs. Cunningham they were eating,

He backed out of there quickly, swinging his stick blind, in case there were any little animals sneaking up on him. He breathed raggedly as he tried to process and believe what he'd just seen.

Fucking squirrels just ate my friends.

He stood, hunched over in the middle of the road, not particularly caring about oncoming traffic. He felt like he was going to turn inside out and spill his lunch on the blacktop. After that, his brains would follow. Rafael stood like that until the screaming in his head went away.

He looked up and through the blood-splattered windshield of the white Escalade. He saw eyes staring back at him, wide, brown eyes in a blood-smeared face. Whoever that was, they had sat in their car and watched the entire time.

Rafael pulled himself up straight and walked over to the passenger side window. He tapped on it with the end of his baton. The spalled window gave off the dull "thunk" of bullet-proof polycarbonate, instead of the higher, clearer sound of safety glass. The man behind the wheel just shook his head.

"Come on out, sir. I need to talk to you."

Rafael wiped some of the mess of the window so he could get a better look.

The Latino man in the red-blotched white suit shook his head more emphatically. Though his fancy haircut and close-trimmed beard looked like he'd been in a knife fight with a hemophiliac, Rafael recognized the face from something back at the office, though he couldn't quite put his finger on it.

As Rafael tried to work out what might the next reasonable step, the sound of an explosion thundered out of the night. He turned and saw a black cloud, momentarily illuminated by fire, rising in the south. From his rough bearings, he'd say it was the Day Farm, where any anti-squirrel action would be most likely to start.

BOWLING FOR RODENTS

K enny hated Thursday nights at the Crickson Starlite lanes. It was Glo Bowling night, when the alleys normally occupied by mildly drunk league bowlers were taken over by semi-lucid senior citizens, their screaming grandkids, and totally hammered college kids.

The house lights were kept down and the black lights cranked up. Grinning spacemen in flying saucers zipped through the stars and planets on the walls, all of them in garish florescent colors. It was enough to make you sick. Beer sales were always off on Glo Bowling nights. The only fun Kenny had on those nights was forensics; bodily fluids, like saliva, semen, what have you, fluoresced the same as the UV paints. Some of the kids coming in from the parking lot had really entertaining stains on their face, hands, and clothes that lit up like fire once they stepped under the black lights. Kenny thought about taking pictures and starting a subreddit site, but that would probably get him fired.

As a toddler in pigtails was at the line of alley number nine, putting both arms and her back into rolling a florescent pink six-pounder down the lane, a ruckus came out of the machinery behind the pins. Kenny watched as the ball slowly zig-zagged down toward the pins between the inflatable bumpers that filled the gutters. Once some pins got knocked down, and the reset mechanism kicked in, he might get a clue as to what happened.

The ball miraculously hit the one pin and plowed through to the seven. As it disappeared down the throat of the ball return, the reset rack came down to retrieve the standing pins and sweep away the fallen. The rack creaked and shuddered as it rose up. It made a screeching noise as it locked up in the top position. Then, little animals starting dropping onto the highly waxed wood of the alley where the pins had been.

As they slipped and tumbled their way up the lanes toward the bowlers, Kenny could see that they were squirrels. Dozens of them. They dropped from the mechanisms behind the other lanes and stumbled their way up the wood ways. The animals' fur was wet and glistened faintly under the black lights, the stains looking black as tar. He had picked up enough UV lore to guess that it was blood.

The little girl stood fascinated at the foul line as the rodents came at her.

"Kitties?" she crooned.

An adult scooped her up, not wanting to see what a herd of frightened or injured squirrels might do to a kid. Some of the near-sober college girls shrieked at the sight of the fluffy little vermin and ran. There was a general retreat to the high ground of the snack bar and the pro shop, not yet a panic.

Kenny pulled out his cell phone and hit the button for the owner. It went straight to voicemail.

One of the college kids held his position at the line, clutching his Day-Glo green ball in his hands, mindless of the squirrels filling his lane. He let fly with amazingly decent form, considering the situation, and stood watching. The ball knocked several squirrels, ass over teakettle, bouncing into the bumpers as it curved into the sweet spot between the one and three pins. All ten pins, along with a few extra squirrels, went down.

"Strike!" he shouted to himself. Most of his buddies had already fled.

The bowler ambled to the ball return to finish off his last frame. He was in his zone. A quick glance at the scoreboard told Kenny that another strike would make this a two-seventy plus game, in spite of the pandemonium around them. The bowler reached into the open maw of the bowl return, wiggling his fingers in anticipation. A bunch of squirrels rushed out of the mechanism ahead of the ball and began chewing his fingers to the bone.

That was enough for Kenny. He locked himself in the office, figuring that he'd be safe. He called the owner again.

"Listen," he told the voicemail beep, "you don't pay me enough to get eaten alive. I quit."

As he tucked the phone into his back pocket, he heard the sound of scurrying feet and realized that the squirrels had gotten into the drop ceilings above him. They chewed their way through the acoustic tile and began dropping into the office, a few at a time.

Just behind him, a giant black-and-tan squirrel landed on top of the league trophy. It was a monster, with multiple gold and marble columns and winged victories perched on top. The squirrel's weight toppled it, and all Kenny could do as it fell was stand and watch the uppermost figure plummet right at his face. The little gold bowling ball it held aloft caught him right between the eyes.

Then, the lights went out.

* * *

"I'm going to need you to come out of the car, sir," Rafael shouted through the bulletproof glass. The man behind the wheel continued to shake his head, either suffering from shock, or sheer cussedness.

Rafael didn't have time for this shit.

He picked up one of the road flares from behind the Escalade and waggled it in front of the windshield to catch the man's attention. He then casually walked it over to the back of Sgt. Chuck's truck and popped open the gas tank cover with his free hand. As Rafael undid the gas cap, the civilian's head shaking became more emphatic, his eyes grew wider.

Rafael stuffed the butt end of the flare down the throat of the gas tank. The fumes didn't catch right off, but there was no saying when it would. He stepped away from wreck, into the grass of the berm. The civilian launched himself out of the SUV.

"Are you out of you fucking mind, *hijo de puta?*"

Rafael smoothly drew his sidearm and aimed it at the center of the blood-spattered man's forehead. "Please step to the back of the car, sir."

The man raised his hands above his head as he backed away.

"With pleasure." He switched his attention between possible obstacles at his feet and the nine-millimeter bore directed at his brain pan. He stopped ten feet behind the white Cadi.

"Now what?"

"Turn around, hands behind your back."

The look on the man's face was priceless. Rafael wished he had a body cam to copy the video for home viewing later.

"Is that really necessary?"

"Considering the circumstances," Rafael said as he clamped the cuffs tight around the man's wrists, "it's the least I could do."

He perp-walked the man to the back of his own SUV and stuffed him in not so gently. Then, Rafael got in behind the wheel and headed for the Day farm. He could see the wrecked vehicles catch fire in his rearview, killing the last of the squirrels in the back seat, and giving Sgt. Chuck the Viking funeral he always deserved.

GRANDMA'S ZONE OF DEATH

Sluggo clipped off another sideview mirror from a parked car as he swerved to avoid a blue SUV backing out of the Quikee Fill.

Bubba, sitting on the side that hit, jumped and shouted at first. He turned to Sluggo and laughed once they were clear. This was how it was when they had gone out bashing mailboxes when they were kids. Hell, they got drunk and did it last month.

He's dinged a few cars in his days of driving a tow truck, and that had always been a pain in the ass in the end. The owners would yell and get paid for repairs, then Sluggo's bosses would chew him out for inattentiveness. It wasn't going to matter tomorrow morning.

The owner of the parked car, they would most likely be eaten by squirrels. That snippy dispatcher at the tow yard, Delia Pearl, squirrels would eat her bony ass, too. His ex-wife, her ponytailed boyfriend, the Humboldt County Sheriff's department; all squirrel chow. It was incredibly freeing to know that everyone

Sluggo hated, and that was pretty much everyone he knew, were going to be eaten by GMO rodents.

Sluggo pegged five more sideview mirrors on the way to the Lucky's parking lot. He was having a hell of a good time with the end of the world.

He parked right at the front of the store, across two handicapped parking spots, just 'cause he knew that would piss some people off, too. Besides, he would be the guy they'd call to tow the truck away, and he wasn't taking any calls tonight. He pointed out their getaway car, a maroon minivan with a *Squirrel in a Blender* bumper sticker from the local radio station, and tossed Bubba the keys.

"Go check out the van," he told his cousin. "Make sure it runs. I'm getting us a case of beer."

"You sure about that?" Bubba asked. It wasn't like his gut was any smaller than Sluggo's, or his record any cleaner. All the gunfire and dead cows and killer squirrels must have just been making him squeamish.

"You take care of business," Sluggo said. "I sure as hell am not going through the rest of the evening stone cold sober."

He went into the grocery and snatched two twelve-packs of Pabst from the cooler. He thought, for just a moment, about simply walking out through the automatic doors, giving Nina the finger as he went, but there might be one of the few cops left in Crickson hanging out at the cafe tonight. The world wasn't quite finished just yet, and he'd hate to be trapped in a cage when a million hungry squirrels arrived.

* * *

Grandma's house looked like pictures Chris had seen of Syria after years of civil war. All around the house, everything less solid than her old pick-up truck had been ground into a fine layer of debris. The few large trees in the forty-foot zone of death looked as slick and polished as baseball bats. The paint on her old pick-up looked like it got sandblasted off on the side nearest the house, and all the glass was shattered. His Range Rover, parked on the far side of it, fared a little better, at least at first glance.

All of her bird feeders and whirligigs were gone. All the flowers and shrubs were shredded. Scattered across all the debris were a million bits of squirrel, made up of wet fur and bone and meat.

"Wow," Dakota said, the first to dare to speak. "Your grandma finally went nuclear."

"I wish I knew what she used," Cesar replied. "Impressive."

Liv, with her wide-eyed, silent expression, seemed to be siding with the two parents in the front seat. They were horrified.

"What the fuck did she do?" Olivia muttered as she slowly pulled up the last few feet into the war zone.

"I'd guess it was a variation on a claymore," Cesar explained, "set to explode outwards with some kind of shrapnel."

Olivia gaped at Chris and then turned around to the kids in the backseat.

"Did any of you know about this?" she asked. "Did you know that she had her house rigged to self-destruct?"

She shifted the car into park, set the brake, and then clutched the wheel as she stared at the desolation.

"I know I'm a lousy parent, but I wouldn't put my baby in a house that might blow up. You believe me, don't you, Chris?"

She sounded neck deep in self-pity and recriminations, a position he was very familiar with.

"I think you're missing the most important thing; the kids are okay, we're okay, and—"

That's when somebody started firing a shotgun on the far side of the house.

Chris dove under the dashboard, out of practiced reflex. Olivia twisted and tried to cover the kids with her body while still buckled in to her shoulder harness. From the sound of their voices, the kids had made a panicked dive for the carpet.

Chris peeked out over the dashboard after the shooting stopped. He couldn't see anyone with a gun, a shotgun from the sound of it, so they probably couldn't shoot him accidentally, either. He unbuckled and got out of the car.

"Grandma!" he shouted as he slowly moved away from Olivia's SUV. "Everything OK?"

Two more shots rang out, and Chris dropped to his knee. There were too many sharp splinters of wood, and other debris, for him to risk throwing himself down belly first.

"Die, you filthy animals!" screeched a familiar voice.

Chris called out her name again, hoping the "filthy animals" were squirrels and not him at the moment.

Grandma came around the corner of the fractured house. She had a pump shotgun in her hands and a bandoleer of ammo across her chest, over a Crickson Dairies sweatshirt.

Imagine Rambo, at eighty-five, in house slippers.

Her knuckles turned white from her grasp on her gun. She suddenly put the butt of it against her shoulder and fired twice into a knot of squirrels on the roof of the garage.

Chris barely had time to react.

"So?" she shouted across to him. "Do you still think I'm crazy?"

"Yes," he shouted back, "but it looks like you were right!"

She shuffled the twenty or thirty feet between them, kicking debris out of her way occasionally with her slippers.

"So are the kids with you?'

"Yes," Olivia said as she came out of the car. "They stole your golf cart and drove into town."

She waved fiercely for the children in the backseat to come out.

They came out with their heads down, black sheep being lead to slaughter. After all, Grandma still had the shotgun.

"You three juvenile delinquents," the old lady snarled. "I should call the cops on you."

Chris heard the faint whine of a police siren in the distance that grew steadily louder. Red and blue lights on the road came from the same direction.

Grandma worked her brows and forehead in deep thought. "Did I call the cops and forget about it?" she asked.

"I don't think you had time," Chris responded.

"We saw your home defense system flash on the horizon," Cesar stated. "I'm sure everyone north of town saw it."

Grandma looked at him sideways, then, at the battered hulk of her home. She nodded absently and ambled down the driveway to await the cops behind Olivia's car.

The rest followed tentatively.

She stood there, gun still in her hands, but muzzle aimed towards the ground, as the Sheriff's Department SUV crept up the driveway. The blue and red lights on top colored everything. Chris stepped a little to his left, both to see who was in the cop car, and to stand clear of their line of fire when they saw the crazy, old lady with the shotgun.

He wasn't sure he was relieved when he saw Rafael step out. There was blood on his hands, and something darker in his eyes. The passenger in the white suit, someone Chris didn't recognize, was covered in blood.

Rafael didn't say anything at first; he just stared back as Grandma glared at him.

Olivia broke and ran though, throwing herself into his arms as he approached. She knocked him back a little with the impact.

"Oh, my God, Raff! I'm so glad to see you!"

She wrapped her arms around him and squeezed. He hugged back, gently patting the back of her head.

"*Tranquillo*," he murmured. "It's going to be okay."

She pulled back. Chris really couldn't see her expression from behind.

"I don't think so," she said. "I think we are all a long way from 'okay.' "

"Could be." Rafael grimaced for just a moment, then put on his "in-control-cop" face they must teach at the academy. "Does anybody really know what's happening?"

"It's squirrels, Tio Rafael," Cesar spoke up. "For some reason, they're going crazy and eating people."

The cop tilted his head to one side to stare down at his nephew.

"Aren't you supposed to be at home right now?"

Cesar slid behind Chris and he swore he could feel Rafael's stare drill its way through his chest. Fortunately, maybe, there were more terrifying things to discuss.

"But, now," Chris said, "you don't have to worry about Cesar being all alone while ravenous killer squirrels are eating anything they can get their paws on."

Rafael scowled from one side of his face, as he always did when faced with a moral dilemma, but then nodded appreciatively.

"You've got a point." He looked around Chris, where Cesar cowered in his shadow. "You're still grounded until after college."

SQUIRREL APOCALYPSE • 137

Dakota stepped forward to draw heat away from his best friend. "So who's this guy?"

Rafael looked over his shoulder at the stranger on the other side of the Sheriff's SUV.

"Him? That's Abraham Vizcarra, murderer, drug-peddler, and general bad *hombre*."

The stranger gaped at Rafael. The reaction wrapped in a blood-spattered white linen suit was hilarious.

"You knew?"

"We do get the bulletins from the DEA." Rafael scoffed. "We're not a bunch of total idiots swilling donuts and coffee, twenty-four seven. Besides, who else would be driving a bullet-proof Cadillac covered with blood and fur?"

He indicated a spot between him and Grandma with a jerk of his chin as he kept his right hand on the butt of his weapon.

"Why don't you step on over here where we can keep an eye on you, all right?"

Vizcarra nodded. He followed orders, walking slowly over toward Chris and his family.

Grandma kept her shotgun aimed in his general direction as he did.

"So," Rafael said, "killer squirrels?"

"That's what the radio reports say," Olivia replied. "We saw some, but didn't hang around long enough to let them kill us."

"I've seen them," Rafael said. "They got Sgt. Chuck Slaybaugh and, I think, Mrs. Cunningham."

"And Mr. Cunningham, along with several of my business associates," Vizcarra added.

"So sorry for your loss." Grandma shifted her weapon to point directly at him.

"So what are we going to do?" Olivia asked. "We can't just wait here."

Rafael surveyed the destruction, whistling low under his breath every once in a while.

"So you got them all in one place and blew them up, Mrs. Day?"

"I'm pleading the Fifth."

Chris chuckled at that.

Olivia was still in frantic mom mode. "But they're going to come back, aren't they?" She scanned the battered branches of trees outside Grandma's Zone of Death. "I mean, there's thousands of them out there, and we can't hide in the house anymore."

"That's the truth." Rafael took up the microphone that dangled from the coiled cable on his chest and clicked the Talk button. "Dispatch, what's your situation there?"

A burst of static came from the radio speaker, but not a word besides that. Rafael clicked the mic a few more times and repeated his message. He gave up after about a half a minute.

Liv stepped forward, fear in her eyes, and steel in her spine.

"What do we do now, Officer Carnicero? We're on our own, aren't we?"

She said exactly what a chivalrous patrolman would want to hear in this situation, exactly in the way he would want to hear it. Chris got a sudden revelation of how often she had played him in the past and how well she had done it.

"Don't be scared, Liv. We'll wait here for a little bit, to see who else might show up, and then get somewhere safe."

"Wait here?" Olivia's tone was getting brittle again, signaling that her nerves might shatter under one more blow. "What kind of idiots are driving around out there, dodging killer squirrels, and navigating by the light of explosions?"

Before anyone could frame a response, two guys in a maroon minivan pulled into the driveway.

WASHOUT

L uke's car already had its wheels in the rails of the carwash when he heard the emergency bulletin. The local station was playing its all oldies format tonight, a steaming mess of Stones and Zeppelin and other crap that had all been recorded decades before he was born. He was about to switch over to the country station when the Voice came on:

"Hate to interrupt your school night date night with David Bowie, but I've been asked to repeat the bulletin by our folks at the Humboldt County Sheriff's Department."

Luke wondered why for a second, since her bulletins were usually who the cops were busting next. Still, he loved the sound of whatever she had to say.

"Swarms of killer squirrels are descending on the town of Crickson, with multiple reports of injury to pets, humans, and livestock. If you are in the Humboldt County area, please close and lock all windows and doors and shelter in place.

"If you see the squirrels in your area, please report them to the Sheriff's Department, or this station. Now, back to David Bowie and 'Ashes to Ashes.'"

At first, Luke thought this was some new promotion. *Be the thirteenth caller after the killer squirrel bulletin and be a winner!* Then he realized that that was a really sucky promotion. They hadn't even mentioned any prizes. So there must be a bunch of rabid squirrels, or a dozen or so that had been eating fermented pumpkins, and they ganged up on somebody's poodle and now there was a panic. People in Crickson didn't know how to handle anything more exciting than the Dairy Festival.

Almost to prove his point, a battered blue van careened down the street behind the car wash. It sideswiped cars in both lanes and sped off out of sight. For that fraction of a second, he could see it, Luke thought he saw little animals hanging off of it.

Maybe there was something to that squirrel announcement after all.

He tried to hand a ten to the scruffy attendant, a flannel-clad figure who looked like he should have been propped up in a cornfield. Luke waved the bill, assuming his visual acuity might be based on motion, and the attendant finally took it and hit the bright red START button. Luke quickly pulled in the sideview mirrors against the car and cranked up the windows before he got dowsed. He felt a gentle lurch as the mechanism grabbed the tires and pulled the car forward at a snail's pace.

There was a less-than-gentle lurch and an almost musical sound of melding plastic and metal that came from behind. Luke cranked his head around to see a red Mustang pressed up against the ass end of his Acura.

I don't believe it, he thought, *some asshole rear-ended me in the goddamned car wash.*

He tried to make out the face of the idiot behind the wheel, but there was something blocking the windshield.

Something that moved.

The car behind his was covered with squirrels. They scratched frantically at the glass and metal and pulled up the wipers to chew on the rubber blades. As every visible space became covered with angry squirrels, some of them skittered forward onto his car. He heard the scratch of claws on the trunk and dozens of footfalls that sounded like hail.

The hood of his car was only just inside the building when the little animals clambered over the glass and tried to gnaw their way in. Luke stepped on the gas before realizing that the car was in neutral and in the grip of the conveyor belt. There was no way out but through at the machinery's pace.

His entire view through the front glass was the pale fur of squirrel's bellies and their brown and yellow teeth as they worked at the glass and molding around it. He heard the klaxon that signaled the initial rinse cycle. He hoped that squirrels didn't like to get wet.

The jets of water didn't dislodge the little bastards. It just made them a little more manic. They started to lose their grip when the nozzles ejaculated thick coils of bluish detergent all over them. The heavy green battens of scrubbing cloth finally dislodged them, slowly pulling rodents off the back side of Luke's car to be dropped into the drainage channels and conveyor belts.

One tenacious squirrel clung for dear life on windshield wipers. The spinning brushes made short work of him. Luke chuckled stupidly through the remaining rinse, buff, and air-dry cycles.

An illuminated red stop sign hung over the exit as the car was pulled to the end of its wash. Once the front tires reached the end of the cycle, the signed blinked out, and a bright green GO sign lit up. No stupid machine had to tell Luke twice.

He put his car in gear and stepped on the gas. The ass end

fishtailed as he made a sharp left turn coming off the rails, and he made a break for freedom. He made it only about twelve feet before he slammed into the ass end of a Jag stopped crosswise across the driveway. Its door was open, and squirrels fed on the bloody arm that dangled out of the car.

"Fuck!" Luke shouted as he pounded on his steering wheel in frustration. There was no way out behind him, and the red Mustang was peeking its nose out of the building, just about to pull out and box him in from behind.

He ran out of time to plan, as the squirrels returned. They had pebbles and acorns in their little paws, ready to make a hundred little star-like cracks in the glass as they pounded their way in.

* * *

"That goddammed bitch!" Sluggo grunted as he poked his head under the back bumper of the minivan. Bubba was down on his knees on the passenger side. A steady drizzle of fluids dripped off the underside to pool in the driveway of the blown-up Day house. It smelled of gas, but also something else that Sluggo couldn't place. It gave him a nightmarish hunch of what might have happened if they hadn't made the side trip to check out the explosion.

Somebody came around to the back side of the car at a leisurely pace, a shadow that craned its neck to look over Sluggo's shoulder at the stream trickling down the driveway.

"Car troubles?" a man said in a smug tone cops usually used at traffic stops.

"I'd say we've got a leak in the gas tank," Bubba replied.

Sluggo looked up and nearly swallowed his teeth when he saw

it was Rafael Carnicero. The last person he wanted to see tonight was that bastard.

"Helluva night," he said as stood and wiped his hands on his overalls. "Eh, Officer Carnicero?"

"Plenty of strange shit going down." The cop nodded and smiled, in a way that showed he was neither happy, nor friendly. "What brings you out in it? Besides a broken-down minivan, that is."

"Us?" Sluggo stitched together as good a lie as he could in the thirteen seconds given to him. "Me and Bubba were driving out to visit our Aunt Eudora in Eureka."

"And did you hit a deer?" Carnicero sniffed the air and then gave both Sluggo and Bubba a dirty look. "Something smells. Smells like bad meat, maybe. Or bullshit."

The cop stepped close to the tail gate of the minivan and jerked his thumb toward passenger side.

"Could you please step away from the car?"

"What?" Sluggo replied.

"Could you *please* step away from the car?"

"Why?"

Carnicero's head cocked over to one side and looked at Sluggo like he was a total fucking moron. "You've seen me work enough times before. Please stand next to your cousin."

Bubba spread his hands, quietly asking Sluggo "What now?"

Sluggo shrugged and scowled as he complied with Carnicero's orders. He really wished he had one of those beers now.

The cop kept an eye on both of them as he crouched down and reached his left hand under minivan's bumper. He brought his hand up in front of his face, rubbing his fingers together and examining them under the flashlight. He held up his red-stained fingertips for all to see.

"This isn't gasoline," he said. Carnicero stared Sluggo right in the eye. "Care to explain why your car is bleeding?"

Sluggo had no idea and couldn't even start to make up a believable story.

Carnicero didn't wait. "Put your hands behind your heads, both of you. Everyone here with shotguns, keep an eye on them. Pretend they're squirrels."

He kept his right hand on the butt of his pistol as he reached for the latch. The cop kept one eye on Sluggo, and the other on the back end of the Odyssey. As he swung up the rear hatch, a stream of bloody fluid flowed out and down over the rear bumper.

Bubba flashed a frightened look at Sluggo, he didn't know what was in the back of the van, either, but he had some pretty scary ideas.

Officer Carnicero stepped back. His expression tightened as he looked over the van's contents. Then, he just looked confused.

"You guys gonna have a really big barbecue down in Eureka?"

Sluggo stepped back up to the car. Carnicero didn't seem as worried about him making sudden moves. Sluggo felt as confused as the cop looked.

What looked like a hundred packs of raw hamburger were stacked in the van. They smelled rotten and bled out a steady stream of fluids that pooled on the floor. Sluggo hadn't noticed the smell before with the scent of bullet-riddled cattle still in his nostrils.

"Sunnuvabitch." Sluggo had a horrifying realization of what the Sciuriologist had in mind for him and his cousin. Looking down the driveway, he saw a trail of blood and gasoline on the pavement that led straight to them.

"Anything you'd like to share with us?" Carnicero asked.

"Yeah," Sluggo muttered. "We've got to get the fuck out of here."

FIVE

ANIMAL RESCUE

Every single dog in the no-kill shelter was going nuts. Some, like the Jack Russell Georgette had named Paco, just spun around in tight circles and yapped up at the ceiling. The pittie with separation anxiety, just rescued from Crickson's only crack house, sat in the corner of her cage, barking and quivering. Elvis, the blue-tick, just bayed loud and low, over and over again.

She had come out into the shelter area as soon as she'd heard about the squirrel invasion on the radio. Georgette heard claws and teeth on the roof once she got out of the office.

A few minutes later, the sound of hundreds of little animals on the roof was like a thunderstorm to Georgette, the two-dozen dogs in their enclosures were like a tornado. She stood just over the drain in the center of the concrete floor. She was trying to come up with a plan, but the noise was driving everything out of her head.

Something hit her in the head. She put a hand up and pulled a few grains of something grey and gritty from her hair.

Plaster dust.

She looked up in time to catch a face full. Georgette spit to clear out the gritty powder in her mouth. She took off her glasses and rubbed them on her shirt to clean off the dust. After that, she squinted up at the ceiling and saw about a dozen holes in the old plaster and lathe ceiling. Each had at least one squirrel snout popping in and out as yellow teeth gnawed at the edges. One squirrel squeezed itself through to plop on the floor near the door to the exercise yard. Another squirrel came through, and then another. Soon, it was a steady stream of rodents that would fill up the room if she didn't do something about it.

The rodents were dropping into the separate enclosures, too.

Paco was grabbing the furry invaders by the necks and killing them as they touched ground. The long-haired dachshund, and the couple of terriers with the same instincts, were stacking up corpses at their feet as quickly as they arrived. Elvis galumphed in circles around his too-small cage, alternating between chasing and being chased. The pit bull still whined and shook as she was cornered by squirrels.

If the dogs were left in their separate cages, Georgette realized, they would all be crushed under the weight of attacking squirrels and gnawed to the bone. Their only hope was *out*.

She popped open Paco's cage first. He danced out, little feet pounding the floor to show his excitement in being outnumbered at least a dozen to one. In his tiny brain, this was a target-rich environment. He went in for the kill even as he was surrounded by angry squirrels nipping at every inch of his wriggling body.

The long-haired wiener dog leaped in to even the odds, turning the fight into a whirling mass of teeth on all sides. The Scotties in the next enclosure, Fitz and Simmons, burst free and joined the fray.

Georgette slogged through the mass of angry animals, opening cage after cage. Squirrels fell on her head and shoulders from the holes in the ceiling as others climbed her legs and nipped through her blue jeans.

It took what seemed forever to get to the last gate and, when she did, the pit bull just cowered in her corner. Georgette tried to coax the dog out, but was interrupted by a sudden shower of plaster and squirrels as the ceiling gave way. The impact drove her to her knees, and the assault of dozens of little bodies, claws, and teeth pushed her the rest of the way to the floor.

As she curled into a ball and folded her arms around her head, she felt the dogs and rodents chase each other over her body. She felt herself being buried in a carpet of blood and fur, and she sincerely hoped that someone would arrive in time to rescue her dogs.

* * *

After a blur of punches, kicks, and angry faces, Sluggo wound up duct-taped to a wooden rocking chair from the porch, right there in the middle of the driveway. His cousin was taped to a folding chaise that looked about to collapse from the weight. Sluggo was pissed.

"You know," Sluggo shouted to no-one in general, "when I told you we had to get out of here right away, I think this is exactly the opposite!"

Cpl. Carnicero stepped into his line of sight with a grim kind of smile on his face. The cop was also holding his nose from where Sluggo slammed the back of his head into it.

"Oh, don't worry, we'll be leaving in just a minute. I just haven't decided whether you'll be coming with us."

Sluggo looked past Carnicero to the three kids who were playing with the raw hamburger packages from the back of his minivan.

"What the hell are those kids doing?" Sluggo looked over at his cousin, Bubba, who was shaking his head like he didn't want to know. The aluminum frame underneath him squealed like it was just seconds away from collapsing.

"We're setting up a transactional framework for contingency management." That was the Latino kid, Carnicero's nephew and some sort of an egghead genius. The kid looked at the two others, who didn't seem to make any more sense of that than Sluggo did. "Motivation. Let's call it 'motivation.'"

The kids went back to work. Now he could see they were laying down a trail of blood and raw meat from the road to him and Bubba.

"If you tell my uncle Rafael what he wants to know," the kid continued, "we'll let you go. Positive reinforcement."

The young girl poured a trail of blood out of one of the hamburger packages, up his leg, and across his chest.

"Refuse to cooperate, and we will leave you here for the squirrels. Negative reinforcement."

"Very negative." The girl took a fistful of the raw meat and stuffed it down the front of his sleeveless T-shirt. Her smile was colder than the hamburger.

"So..." Rafael leaned up against the maroon mini-van and crossed his arms. "What do you two guys know about meat-eating squirrels?"

"Have you all been smoking something?" Sluggo replied. "I don't know what you're talking about."

The other boy, the white pudgy one, started giving Bubba the hamburger treatment. His cousin began to snivel when the cold blood got dribbled on his crotch.

"Oh, God, we're sorry. We didn't know!"

"Didn't know what?" Carnicero asked quickly.

"Bubba doesn't know shit," Sluggo shouted. "He's a freaking retard. Shut up, Bubba!"

"But the deputy says people are dying out there," Bubba whimpered. "And it's all our fault!"

"Just shut up, Bubba!" Even though Sluggo was closing to blacking out as he strained against the tape that held him to the chair, he saw a sly look in Carnicero's eye.

"If you did something wrong, Bubba," he said, "the only way to make it right is to tell the truth. Don't listen to your cousin over there."

"She said it was just a prank," Sluggo sobbed. "She was going to fill the town with squirrels and drive people nuts. She didn't tell us these were meat-eating squirrels!"

"And who is she?" Carnicero was calm, almost friendly now.

"We never knew her name. She called herself the cereal-ologist"

"The what?" The girl asked.

"Sciuriologist," the corporal's nephew declared. "It's a person who studies squirrels."

"You knew that off the top of your head?" the girl asked.

"It was on my summer reading list for AP Biology."

Carnicero ruffled the boy's hair and turned back to Bubba. "I'm so proud of that boy. Now, where is this Sciuriologist, and where does she keep her squirrels?"

"Sluggo, you'd better shut—" Sluggo wasn't able to get any

other words out through the wad of raw hamburger the girl jammed into his mouth. He glared at her and then started chewing. Raw or not, free beef is still free food.

"She lives in the abandoned missile silo on the federal land up north," Bubba said. "The whole place is a gigantic nest."

"And you lead those squirrels into town with a trail of blood?" Carnicero's boy asked.

"Yeah, a truck full of dead cows. They were bleeding."

"So how do we lead them away from town?" Grandma Day asked. "I mean, once we get them away from Crickson, we could dump a ton of napalm on them and have a barbecue."

"I can't see where anything will distract them from all the food available there." Carnicero's nephew said. "They would probably stay put until the local resources were exhausted."

"Those 'resources' are called 'people,' " Olivia told the boy.

"Yeah, sucks to be them," the young girl replied.

Sluggo had finally swallowed the plug of hamburger he'd been chewing, and he laughed out loud at the girl's sass.

Olivia spun toward her with a parental fire flashing from her eyes.

"Listen here, Liv," she said, "just because we're in a bit of a difficult situation, that's no excuse for that kind of attitude."

"Give her a break," one of the other men said, probably her dad. "She's just scared. She acts out when she's scared."

"She walks all over you," Olivia snapped back.

Then, the lot of them started yelling at each other. Some of them were waving shotguns. Sluggo started scooting his rocking chair away from the fracas.

"I may have an idea!" somebody shouted.

The yelling did not quiet down one bit.

The same somebody slammed fists on the hood of the minivan, over and over, while howling out a long stream of obscenities in Spanish. Sluggo picked up a few words, something about his mother and a goat with brass balls.

Carnicero waved everyone into silence.

They turned to look at the Mexican cop in the blood-spattered white suit.

"I know what attracts the squirrels."

"What?" Grandma Day asked.

"They are very defensive," Carnicero said. "If you attack them, they will go to great lengths to render you harmless."

"Are you sure?" his nephew asked.

"I ordered some of my men to fire upon them. The squirrels ate them first." The blood-spattered man shrugged.

"Does that make any sense?" The cop asked his boy.

"Whoever bred these animals would really have to ramp up their attack instincts to weaponize them. Otherwise, they'd scatter in all directions at the first instance of counterattack."

Then, Grandma Day's face lit up. "So all we have to do is shoot at them and run away real quick?"

The kid shrugged. "I guess so."

"Then, I've got just the thing for that." The old woman grinned. "Come see what I've got in the garage."

The whole lot of them followed her to the old building covered in drying squirrels' skins, completely forgetting about the two guys they left duct-taped to chairs and covered in blood and hamburger.

ANTI-SQUIRREL INSURGENCY

Her producer dropped a sheaf of yellow call memos on Ellen's broadcast desk during the commercial break.

"From the calls coming in," Anneke said, "there are rabid, killer squirrels *literally* everywhere in town."

She didn't show any sign of panic in her voice, just a tone of tired annoyance. Like air traffic controllers, live radio producers had to have ice water in their veins. As Ellen remembered, this was the same tone of voice Anneke had when the lobby was filled with armed DEA agents last month.

Ellen riffled through the notes. Squirrels at the feed store. Squirrels in the library. Even squirrels in the Nut House, the boutique that sold only nuts, but the little rodents were going after the cashiers instead of cashews.

"I'll break in again and let the people know."

"Break in?" Anneke asked. "I think this would warrant cancelling our 'regularly scheduled programming.'"

"And give up my tribute to George Michael?"

Anneke gave her the look, the one she shot through the

sound-proof glass when Ellen had overstepped the station's bounds.

Ellen grimaced back. "All right, we're on emergency broadcasting right after the commercial."

Ellen wheeled her chair over to the outside window. The studio was on the top floor of the Krieger building, at seven floors the tallest in downtown Crickson. The streets below looked like a Warner Brothers version of Dante's *Inferno*.

People were running and waving their hands, as they were pursued by legions of flesh-eating squirrels. The screams didn't make it through the triple-pane window. Cars swerved in and out through the chaos. Some ran down squirrels, one tagged a panicked man in a flannel shirt and sent him flying onto the sidewalk. One of the sheriff's cruisers had rolled over on its side. Black smoke oozed out from under its hood.

These people didn't need her to tell them that hell had broken loose in Crickson. Those who could hear her probably needed soothing music, just like the dance band on the Titanic playing hymns as the passengers fought to get on the lifeboats. But the FCC would disagree, same as Anneke, and Ellen would like to have a job tomorrow when the dust had settled.

She was just about to wheel back to her microphone when she saw something strange. It looked like battle wagon from a Mad Max movie with corrugated steel bolted onto all sides and the top. Heavy steel mesh covered the windshield. The improvised tank stopped in the middle of the street, and a hatch popped open on the top. Somebody in a welder's mask and heavy gloves appeared like a jack-in-the-box and started taking pot shots at the squirrels with a shotgun.

It didn't seem to have any effect. Any squirrels shot were replaced by several more angrier squirrels. In the span of a single commercial, the little animals gathered around the battle wagon, practically covering the sidewalks with fur.

The shooter slapped the roof of corrugated steel three times and disappeared back down the hatch. The armored car careened down the street before the hatch had even sealed. The squirrels pursued, covering the road like an angry carpet with teeth.

Ellen rolled back to her mic. She was ready to do her part in communications in the war against the squirrels. She wasn't entirely sure there was going to be a tomorrow for her and the radio station.

* * *

"Reload!" Chris's grandmother dropped a shotgun into his hands as the hydraulics on her swivel chair dropped her below the level of the reinforced roof. "There's plenty more squirrels to piss off out there."

The gun was still hot from firing. Chris juggled it a bit until he could get it laid on the floor and refilled with shells.

Bubba, or Sluggo, he couldn't tell them apart, handed her a fully loaded twelve gauge and then braced himself against the gee-forces of the turn.

Rafael was driving this armored sled like he had stolen it. Some part of the armor came loose and dropped to the street on the turn.

"Grandma," Chris shouted, "when I built this for you, it was to take us to Burning Man, not combat!"

The old lady guffawed and swiveled from side to side, duct-taped into her seat for a steady shot.

"Do you really think I would be caught dead at that desert deviant festival?" she shouted back. "If I told you I was preparing for when squirrels threatened humanity, you would have put me away!"

The sled hit a series of bumps at high speed, probably a rail crossing. Chris went airborne for a moment and crashed back to the floor.

"That is still an option," he shouted, "if there is still an 'away' to put you tomorrow!"

Chris glanced back at Liv and the others. She, of course, looked like her normal, sullen self. The boys were wide-eyed with terror, but Olivia looked like a mama grizzly with her arms wrapped protectively around Dakota.

"Of course," he said for their benefit, "everything is going to work out just fine. Trust me."

Liv grimaced. "That's the same tone of voice you used when you said you and Mom weren't getting a divorce."

"That was different."

Before he had a chance to say anything more, Chris lifted off from the floor and flew forward to bounce off the back of the passenger's seat. Everyone but Grandma, who was strapped in, took pretty much the same trajectory and piled up near the front as the sled came to a sudden stop.

"A little warning would be nice!" the old lady shouted from her swivel chair.

"The street's blocked," Rafael yelled back over his shoulder, "and, even with all this dead weight, I don't think we could plow through it!"

"Is he calling us dead weight?" one redneck asked the other.

"We're not dead yet."

Chris pulled himself to standing on back of the seat and helped Olivia and Liv to their feet. The boys, somehow, had bounced over everyone else and wound up wedged cheek to jowl between the front seats.

Rafael's prisoner, or whatever, Vizcarra, was pressing his eye to the glass behind the armor slit on his side. He sounded pretty disturbed when he finally spoke up. "Your mission to piss off all the killer squirrels in the vicinity seems to have been a success. There are several hundred of those vicious little bastards on my side."

Grandma dropped down the military surplus tanker's periscope from the hatch above her head. Holding the flat optic box to her eyes, she swiveled a full three hundred and sixty degrees to scope out their surroundings.

"Yep," she said. "They're coming at us from all sides."

"I'm sure that's supposed to be good news," Chris muttered. "Where do we go from here?"

Grandma slammed the periscope shut. "I think I have an idea."

GOT MILK?

afael wanted to bang his head against the steering wheel. His town was on fire and filled with killer squirrels. The windshield view was quickly filling up with the view of their furry bellies as they tried to chew their way in. Everyone he cared about, Cesar, Chris the man he waited twenty years for, even Olivia, were locked in this metal box on wheels as bait. On top of it all, that smug son of a goat Vizcarra sat in the passenger seat and grinned.

"Now, you see why I did not want to come out of my car?" The drug boss tried to wipe a speck of blood off his sleeve, but only made it worse.

"Are you sure about this, Mrs. Day?" Rafael shouted over his shoulder.

"Definitely! A dairy tanker will have way more carrying capacity and... oomph."

"We will need oomph."

"So what are sitting here for?" Bubba grunted from the floor.

Rafael stepped on the clutch and the gas to rev this armored sled as much as it could go.

"Hang on to your last meal, folks."

He kicked it into first and rushed toward the barricade of wrecked vehicles. With a foot or two to spare, he pushed the van into a bootleg turn that swung its tail end around clockwise until they were aimed the way they came. He gunned the engine and sped down the street to make another turn the opposite way.

He could hear bodies tumbling around in the back as he pulled these maneuvers, along with a lot of shouting and swearing. The squirrels squealed, too, as they lost their grip on the wire mesh over the windshield and flew off into the night. He could feel the minute bumps as he drove over their furry asses on his way to the Sunny Day Dairy on the edge of town.

He serpentined through the streets, avoiding debris and wrecked cars. And bodies. There were a few red smears on the road surrounded by knots of flesh-eating squirrels. Those he actually swerved to run over, picking them off like extra points in a game of *Spy Hunter*.

The dairy loomed up in front of them, a low brown brick building with details in bright green and yellow. A gigantic roll-up door large enough to accommodate three semis side-to-side took up the nearest wall.

"Mrs. Day," Rafael shouted over his shoulder. "Do you have some sort of opener for this door? I sure don't want to step outside."

"It's the long pedal on the right," she shouted back.

It was a stupid idea, but the best response he could think of with a herd of flesh-eating squirrels on their tails. He leaned right, and left, to get the best view through the scratches and droppings left on the windshield and floored it.

"Everybody, hold on to something!"

Vizcarra crossed himself and muttered prayers to the Mother

of God and Santa Muerte. The lot in the back made the appropriate noises for a group that had several seconds to think about a crash.

The engine roared and knocked like a wounded animal.

The bright green slats of the roll-up door filled his view, and Rafael prayed that they wouldn't simply bounce off.

Everything went black at the moment of impact.

The yards of flexible metal made a sound like a gong as the armored van hit them. The protective metal screen over the front glass peeled off as the van punched through. The corrugated steel on the front went with it. It sounded like fingernails on chalkboard as it did.

The van made it a few yards into the building and jerked to a stop. The passengers inside kept going for a fraction of a second. Chris wound up on his back between the two front seats.

"What the hell happened?" he asked as he slid back from the engine cover and rubbed the lump on his forehead. "Well, we punched through, but the roll-up door peeled the sheet metal off this sled like a big steel banana." Rafael experimentally applied some pressure on the gas pedal, but only got the squeal of rubber against concrete in return. "And, now, we're stuck."

"But at least the front end is inside the building," Mrs. Day said in an entirely too cheerful tone. Duct-taped into her swivel chair, she was the only one, besides himself and Vizcarra, who hadn't gotten bounced around like ping-pong balls in a lottery machine. She cut herself free as everyone else was cataloguing their injuries.

Rafael unbuckled and checked out the best angle to kick the windshield out of its frame. He had his right foot set between Chris's face and Vizcarra's leg and his left up on the dashboard when Mrs. Day shouted at him to stop.

"What?" Rafael shouted back. He had to hang on to the

steering wheel to keep from falling on top of Chris.

The old woman held up a white plastic spray bottle in each hand.

"Before anyone goes out there," she said, "I've got to dowse them in squirrel repellent."

* * *

Chris swore that the cloud of stench escaping the van had a mouth and eyes, just like a cartoon ghost. It looked horrified, or disgusted, but that might have just been the burning and watering of his eyes. It could have been the oxygen being cut off to his brain by shallow breathing through his mouth, alternating with groans of anguish.

Whatever it was, the stench seemed no happier with itself than his family was with the experience of concentrated varmint repellant.

"One hundred per cent American fox urine," Grandma proclaimed proudly as she applied it to every inch of the van's passengers. "Fermented for extra strength!"

Chris went out the gap where windshield had been, rolling down the hood of the van to land on the concrete like a sack of feed. He gilled like a fish out of water for a few moments. The cool concrete felt soothing on his cheek. Then his vision cleared, and he looked down the length of the underside of the armored sled. A single squirrel crept in through the gap under the van. It moved forward cautiously, sniffing the air as it went. It got within a few feet of Chris and began blinking and shaking its head violently from side to side, as if it were in pain.

Chris lifted off of the floor, partially from pure adrenaline, the rest from having the two rednecks pulling him up by his arms.

"We've got to get out of here right now," he shouted. "Those rodent bastards are coming in under the van."

Rafael was right at his elbow as soon as Sluggo/Bubba released him.

"Already? How many were there?"

"Just one or two. They're busy vomiting under the differential from the smell, but that won't occupy them for long."

Rafael clapped his hands for attention. "Okay, kids, we have to leave right now. Double time!"

The adults pulled the children through the punched-out windshield, gently placing them, feet-first, on the cement floor. That left only Grandma. Chris was reaching up to help her down when she leaped though the gap, hit the ground in a tuck, and rolled back onto her feet in a single motion. She held a white spray bottle of repellant in either hand.

"Have you been skydiving again, Grandma?"

"Not for the last year or so," she shouted over her shoulder, "but, yeah."

She franticly pumped away at the concrete around the van to lay down a chemical barrier against squirrels. Chris heard angry-sounding chirps and clicking of teeth from underneath, maybe even the quiet noise of tiny animals retching. He could understand that. The unmitigated stank rising from his body was still enough to make his eyes water.

"That will slow them down," the old lady muttered, "but it won't keep them out forever. What I wouldn't give to blow *all* their sorry asses up."

His mind flashed back to his work in the dairy a week or two ago. "I might be able to do something along those lines."

His grandmother beamed up at him. "What do you have in mind?"

UNDER PRESSURE

R afael watched Olivia, Mrs. Day, and the kids on top of the refrigerated tanker with no little concern. It was stupid, but it would still be a tragedy if anyone fell and broke their necks instead of being eaten.

Olivia opened the topside hatch and peered inside. She pulled back with a grimace of disgust. "Gawd!" she said. "It smells like rancid cheese in there!"

"You don't exactly smell like a packet of Summer's Eve, yourself," Mrs. Day responded.

The kids gaped and exchanged mortified expressions.

"Did your grandmother just call my mom a douche?" Dakota asked Chris's daughter.

Cesar leaned in close to Dakota. "I think that is exactly what she *wasn't* trying to say."

Rafael pressed his fist against his lips to suppress the laughter that would only encourage more nonsense.

"Enough horseplay," Rafael shouted. "Just get in the can. The squirrels will be in here any second!"

164 • JOSEF MATULICH

The women lowered the children in, one at a time, and then Olivia helped Mrs. Day down.

"No parajumping," she warned, "You'll break a hip."

"You're all a bunch of wusses. Watch out that you don't break a nail."

The old woman dropped from sight, landing with a faint splash and a metallic "clang."

Olivia took a moment to aim a troubled glance Rafael's way and follow her into the dairy tanker. That left Bubba and Sluggo in the truck cab. Vizcarra was just outside, where Rafael could keep an eye on him, and Chris.

Chris was nowhere to be seen.

"Chris!" Rafael called out. "We don't have time for hide and seek."

Rafael had spent his life hiding his feelings, especially from himself. He wasn't going to go all touchy-feely in the midst of a disaster. He scratched his head franticly behind his right ear, a nervous tic he developed shortly after taking Cesar into his home, and called out again.

A few seconds later, Chris came loping around the back of the truck like a scrawny, blonde coyote. "Not so loud," he stage whispered. "You'll attract squirrels, *pendejo*."

Rafael did not rise to the taunt. "You okay?"

"No," Chris said. "We need to get out of here in, maybe, the next forty-five seconds."

"What, now?"

Chris pointed behind him. "On the other side of this truck is a fifty-year old refrigeration compressor. I saw some squirrels over there dicking around with the hoses and valves."

"And..."

"And, in about sixty seconds, they're all going to become flying squirrels."

Rafael's stomach did a back flip. "You're saying that the fucking squirrels set off the dairy to explode?"

"If any insurance adjusters come around asking questions, that'll be what I say."

Chris hightailed it to the ladder at the back of the tanker trailer. "This will probably take out half the rodents in town, but I definitely do not want to hang around to watch."

Rafael dashed up to the semi-tractor, where Sluggo and Bubba were lounging around like they were on a union-mandated break.

"You wanted to drive the big rig?" he shouted. "Get in and drive!"

Sluggo was slow to respond. He still leaned back on the driver's side fender. "What's the hurry? We're safe in here."

"No, we're not!" Chris shouted as he sat on the edge of the hatch to lower himself into the tanker. A high-pitched squealing noise came from the compressor.

"Not helpful, Chris! In about thirty seconds, we are going to die from an industrial accident instead of squirrel bite." Rafael climbed on top of the truck's hood and eyeballed their approach to the doors opposite the one they punched through earlier. "We're too close to get up any speed to ram. Pull us right up to the door so I can hit the switch."

"You nuts?" Bubba asked as he waddled over to the passenger side and began the ponderous task of climbing up to the height of the cab.

"Desperate, and depending on you to save us all." He pulled the baton from the ring on his belt, just in case he would need to crack some tiny skulls. "That makes me stupid, too."

"No need to get nasty," Sluggo said as he slid behind the wheel.

"Drive or die, *gallita*."

Sluggo fired up the engine, filling up the hall with a rumble like thunder and clouds of black exhaust. The screech from the compressor kept getting louder and, now, the machine shuddered like it was coming apart. With a grinding noise that shot up Rafael's spine, the truck dropped into gear and crawled up to the roll-up door. The switch for the motors hung from an inch-thick cable.

Rafael snagged it and pulled up the switchbox to his own level. With a prayer to Mother Maria, he hit the big green button etched with the word UP.

The gigantic door, the size of a whole wall of his apartment building, shook and then noisily crawled upwards at a snail's pace. Rafael stayed at the switch, in case something went wrong.

The door kept rising, but slowly. It only moved about a foot during the first few seconds.

The squirrels came much faster.

Maybe a dozen of them slipped under the door in that time. They sniffed around the floor, not yet noticing the snack tray standing on the hood. Rafael casually lowered the switch to the end of its tether, trying to not make any sudden movements that might attract attention. He let it go and very, very slowly climbed down backwards toward the door.

He froze when he heard squealing and chattering behind him. Out of the corner of his eye, he could see squirrels raising a commotion on the van and the floor beneath it. He didn't know what the noises meant, but they all seemed to be pointing at him with their paws and noses.

Those little bastards ratted me out, Rafael thought.

The squirrels on the floor beneath the truck all raised their heads and focused on him like he was a bag full of peanuts. They bounced toward him, making all kinds of vicious noises he didn't know squirrels could make.

Fuck this!

He hunkered down to back off of the hood and onto the running board. With a bit of luck, he could open the door and slip into the cab without getting eaten like Sgt. Chuck. He was halfway down, reaching backwards with one foot for the running board, when something totally unlike a squirrel landed on the hood. It was black and tan, like a Doberman, and about the size of an over-fed raccoon. It bared its teeth, wolf's canines along with rat's incisors, growled like an angry pit bull, and leaped straight for Rafael's face. He went over backwards and hit the concrete hard.

Rafael was stunned from the landing. He was twice-stunned when the beast landed on his chest. It sank its teeth into the left side of his face and chin, pulling back for just a moment, no doubt from the taste of fox urine that covered Rafael.

The pain brought things into focus.

He swatted the animal away with his baton and brought up his left arm and elbow to protect his throat and the other side of his face. Other squirrels clambered onto his prone body, and they sounded angry at him fighting back. They were really no bigger than kittens, but there were at least a dozen of them. Sharp squirrel teeth tore little furrows in his clothes to expose the skin underneath. Every bite burned like fire.

Rafael flailed blindly with the baton and rolled over his attackers. He hoped stop, drop, and roll worked on squirrels. Every time he moved, more squirrels piled on and used their sharp claws and teeth. Rafael was collapsing under the weight of a million cuts when everything went white.

He was suddenly cold, like skinny dipping in a stream of fresh snow-melt. A strangely acrid taste filled his mouth as the cloud that surrounded him got inhaled. He might have tried to spit it out if he weren't still screaming about being eaten by squirrels. Then, he realized the little bodies were no longer clinging to his. He felt human hands grab him and lift him.

Without any resistance, or volition, he flopped into a padded seat. The truck door slammed, and all the squirrels got sealed on the outside. All but the one that had its teeth sunk into Rafael's pant leg. Somebody grabbed it and pounded it against the dashboard until it stopped being a problem.

Some well-trained part of his brain knew he was going into shock. The other parts closer to the squirrel-torn surface no longer felt the cuts and scratches. He was simply confused why he was still alive.

"What the FUCK just happened?"

Chris leaned forward into the space between the seats and held up a red cylinder. "Fire extinguisher. Behind a little door on the side of the sleeper. It always works in the movies."

Rafael felt suddenly overcome with admiration and gratitude. And blood loss on top of a possible concussion. He unsteadily leaned his head toward Chris's.

"You saved my life. That's so... beautiful." He pointed at Chris, though the finger did not hold steady on his oldest friend. "I love you, man."

"So I've been told."

"What?" Rafael slurred.

Chris was turning pink. Sluggo, Bubba, and Vizcarra were all gaping at him.

Rafael knew that there had been some significance to what had been said, he just couldn't make any connections in his battered brain.

Then, Chris looked out the windshield and practically screamed. "WHAT are we doing still inside the exploding the dairy processing plant?"

Sluggo grimaced and threw the truck into gear. "Sorry," he said, "I guess I got kind of distracted."

The truck chugged forward slowly, out through the lot and probably onto the road. Rafael lost track of things after that as the truck's motion, and his injuries rocked him to sleep.

EARTH-SHATTERING KABOOM

O f course, Chris had no idea when the compressor would blow. Not exactly. It wasn't like setting a nuclear reactor to overload in the movies, with a convenient countdown clock. The old machine's complaints under pressure, which rose constantly in pitch and volume, were close enough. That, and the not-distant-enough sounds of rivets popping off the pressure vessel and ricocheting around the ductwork.

"Can you step on it? That thing is going to explode any second now." Chris was in some trucker's sleeping compartment with Rafael and that was not how he wanted to die.

"Keep your pants on!" Sluggo hollered over his shoulder. "This thing is like a freight train. It does take a little time to build up your momentum."

The overweight redneck set his seed company gimme cap on his head and looked back at Chris in the rearview mirror.

"So what did you mean when you said that you were told that the corporal loved you?" Sluggo asked.

Chris just knew that slip up would never go away.

"Are you really asking about that right now? Just keep your eyes on the road and concentrate on getting us out of this a—"

Chris couldn't even hear himself completing that sentence, as his grandmother's dairy converted itself into a rapidly expanding cloud of bricks, metal, and super-cooled ammonia. At the distance of a couple of hundred yards, the dairy tanker was not swallowed up in that cloud. Chris did hear the machine gun sound of debris pinging off of the metal tank. The trailer's backside swung from side to side, like a drunk stripper on a bar performing for quarters. Sluggo swore and screamed and pulled on the wheel to keep the whole rig from rolling over onto its side. Chris kept a hand pressed down on Rafael's chest to hold him in one place.

The rig finally fell under Sluggo's control, and he popped it into neutral and took his foot off the gas. He and his cousin panted and wheezed as the truck coasted to a stop.

"Jesus fucking Christ!" Bubba groaned.

Sluggo nodded mutely.

"We almost got ourselves killed," Bubba shouted as he twisted around in his seat toward Chris. "You could have warned us."

"I swear I heard myself mentioning an exploding compressor at least twice." Chris felt a strange feeling of icy serenity coming over him. "And as far as nearly being killed, me and my loved ones have been nearly killed two or three times. Because of you two."

Rafael was barely conscious, but he didn't resist when Chris reached across his body and popped his sidearm out of its holster. It felt incredibly heavy as he held it up for the two cousins to see.

"Get us to that silo. Now."

Bubba swiveled around to stare straight ahead through the windshield.

Sluggo popped the truck into gear without a word.

Chris laid the gun down, and Rafael placed a hand over it. With his other hand, he beckoned with one finger.

Chris leaned in closer to hear what his friend had to say.

"Not a bad job," Rafael whispered, "*pendejo.*"

* * *

Sometime during the drive, Chris had laid down next to Rafael, just to rest his eyes. He woke up instantly when he heard a metallic crash.

"What the hell was that?" he called out.

"We just went through the front gate," one of the cousins responded. Chris couldn't tell which one just by sound. "It's only about a hundred yards to the silo."

As the diesel engine roared, and gravel crunched beneath the rig's tires, Chris rubbed his forehead and tried to plot out their next steps. the Voice was playing on the radio, and he wasn't even interested.

"There are more reports of squirrel-related attacks in the downtown area. Avoid Lucky's and the video store. We have confirmed reports of an explosion destroying the Sunny Day Dairy."

First thing, he'd have to do is to see if Rafael was even able to stand. He had been literally chewed up by the little animals. His uniform was shredded, and one eye was swollen shut from cuts across the eyelid. If he was unable to go any farther, they would commandeer his gun and Taser and leave him behind in the truck. There was an axe handle in the sleeping compartment that either Sluggo, or Bubba, could use. Then, they'd have to fish the others out of the tanker trailer. That wasn't going to be easy.

"Flaming squirrels from that explosion have caused scattered fires across the northwestern neighborhoods. Authorities are unable to respond."

Chris fought the response to pound himself in the forehead after hearing that. In the movies, the big explosion always gets rid of the monsters. He, instead, had put half of Crickson to the torch. Maybe it was a good thing that they didn't find a fuel tanker to dump its contents into the squirrels' lair. God knows what kind of damage he could have done.

"We're here," one of the cousins said.

A whirring sound started, what Chris assumed was a cooling fan for the diesel engine now that it had stopped.

It was possible they could drop the semi-tractor into the silo and set the fuel tanks ablaze. Convection and fuel might produce an effect like a blast furnace. But that would only be worthwhile once the squirrels had all come back to their nest. He wasn't even sure that would happen.

As he worked out schemes for squirrel annihilation, the whirring became louder. Chris heard the final three words from the cousins.

"Jesus Fucking Christ."

The whirring sound was replaced with a low rumbling buzz, like the sound of a five-hundred-pound bumblebee flying overhead. Chris heard the windshield shatter, and the men upfront, scream. The fiberglass walls above him shattered as something whizzed over his head and punched quarter-sized holes in everything.

Chris, by reflex, started to raise his head to look, but Rafael's hand in the middle of his chest kept him down. He looked over and saw that the deputy may have been chewed up, but he was far from dead. The look in his eyes was equal parts terror and rage.

"Stay down," he said through gritted teeth.

The gunfire went on for a few seconds more, almost cutting off the cab of the truck at a line just above the dashboard. Then the noise stopped, to be replaced by the sound of a PA speaker, "I should have known you'd come, Iris," a woman's voice said. "Come on down and see what I've done for you."

INSIDE THE TANK

At first, Iris was ready to kill some her people when she saw the condition of the tanker. Whether they were just layabouts that knocked off earlier, or they were chased off by squirrels, they never cleaned out the stainless-steel tank. Gallons of diluted milk, on its way to becoming cheese, remained, enough fluid to make a splash when she dropped down into it. Cracking and shaking the chemical light wands in her squirrel survival kit, she inspected their new surroundings.

The kids looked like glowing mushrooms in the greenish phosphorescence. Olivia looked worse. She breathed rapidly through her mouth because of the smell and her anxiety. She looked like an overheated golden retriever.

"In case we all don't get out of this," Iris said, "there is one thing I want to tell you."

They all turned to face her. Chris sat on the edge of the hatch above, looking down.

"I was right. All along. You thought I was an obsessed old bat with too many guns and too much time on my hands, but I was right."

The kids rolled their eyes at her, the way the younger generation always did.

Olivia gaped at her like she'd been hit in the face with a shovel.

"Do we really need to go there, Grandma?" Chris asked from above.

"I'd just like some validation before we're all torn to pieces by squirrels."

"Nobody's getting torn to pieces on my watch." Chris pulled himself to standing and started to close the hatch. "You all get comfortable. I'll have you out in just a little bit."

He closed the hatch and dogged down the latches. The inside of the tanker was abyssal darkness, broken only by the glow of the chem light and its reflections on the mirror-bright cylinder's walls.

Olivia spread her hands and smiled the way the best moms do to put a good face on a bad situation. "We might as well sit down before we all get knocked down," she said.

She settled down as high up the curving wall as she could. She still slid down until her sneakers submerged in the milk and water at the bottom. She held out one arm to her son, and he curled up beside her. His little Mexican friend curled up on her other side. She wrapped them both up in her arms.

"Just consider this an adventure." She smoothed Dakota's hair with her hand and kissed his forehead. "Like a dark waterslide filled with milk."

Liv stood on the other side of the milk puddle, calculating, like always. She finally opted to sit on Iris's side of the tanker. She didn't sit close enough to be coddled, or cuddled. Separate and untouchable, sort of like Iris for the last forty years.

Iris handed her the chem light, as if it were a family heirloom being passed along.

"Here, you take it. I might drop it in the milk. We don't want to go fishing around in that."

It was impossible to keep in one place once the truck got started. The first jerk as it caught in first gear pulled everyone in the tank toward the back and then forward again. Once the rig had picked up speed, everyone slowly slid toward the rear.

Olivia tried to stick to the stainless-steel walls, palms down, and fingers splayed as if that would generate enough suction to hold her in place.

Iris tried the same without the absolute desperation.

The kids, they gave up and pretended they were at a water park. Knees up and with their hands behind their heads, they slid around in the rancid milk like balls in a lotto machine.

"What the hell," shouted Liv as she slid down the tube, "maybe this will wash off the smell of fox pee!"

Not likely, Iris thought, *but they might as well have their fun.*

There was a sound like thunder, and it felt like a giant hand grabbed the dairy tanker and shook it. Iris got launched across the tank into Olivia, and they both fell, face first, into the fluid that frothed like the worst milkshake ever concocted. The children slid and bounced from back to front and halfway up the sides of the cylinder. Several sounds like gunfire preceded holes appearing in the back end of the shell. The bright light of fire and smoke came though.

A few chunks of something hard came through the stainless-steel wall and slid around the tank with assorted scratching noises. Iris's whole world tumbled around her like a cycle in a spin dryer. Everything spun, everything screamed. One of the children shrilly cursed in what sounded like many different languages.

After a few very long minutes, the ride calmed down. The fluid leaked out through one of many holes, leaving them high and dry like the aftermath of a shipwreck.

"What the FUCK just happened?" Liv shouted at the top of her lungs. Her voice echoed off the steel walls over and over.

Olivia asked the more maternal question, "Is everyone all right?"

"Yeah, Mom," Dakota sputtered. "At least, I think I am."

"Me, too." Cesar held up one of the pieces of debris that had punched through the tank. "Somebody get me the light. Please."

Somebody scuttled along the floor to retrieve the chem light, then they all huddled to examine Cesar's find. It was no bigger than Iris's palm, a bit of pipe and mechanisms.

"It's an old refrigerant pressure valve," Cesar said. "My God, the whole dairy must have blown up!"

"I hope it took every squirrel in town with it," Iris replied.

Olivia looked sideways at Iris with her mouth scrunched one way and her hair pasted to the side of her head with rancid milk. She didn't look entirely convinced.

"I had nothing to do with it. I saw some of those furry little bastards screwing around with the compressor controls when we climbed into the tank here," Iris lied. "You don't believe me?"

"What were those explosive booby-traps you installed around your house again?"

Iris didn't answer, and Olivia didn't really seem to want to know. She looked up and through the holes in the steel liner that shone in the dark like stars in the evening sky.

"I would think the guys would want to come back here and check on us," Olivia said after several quiet moments.

The truck engine rumbled, and they all felt the jerk as the rig started off again.

"I would think not," Liv observed.

"Probably want to get away from the flesh-eating squirrels," Iris added.

The girl settled down on the floor beside Iris, needing warmth and comfort more than her twelve-year old need for independence. Iris pulled her great-granddaughter close with one arm as the rig built up speed and rocked them both to sleep.

Liv was dreaming of her mother when the bullets started flying. She couldn't remember what had scared her so much, something about Mom taking her away and selling her organs on the black market. When she opened her eyes, there was something to really be scared about.

Something punched holes in the big tin can they rode in, through and through, like a cyborg woodpecker with a titanium beak going postal on them. Liv couldn't do anything but lie on her back and cover her ears. The sounds of dozens of impacts went through her head like the bullets.

Grandma was always ready for anything. As the rest of them froze, she started yelling for everyone to get down. She pulled people down if they didn't act like they heard her. All Liv knew for certain was that she was lying, face down, in the lowest part of the milk tanker with Grandma's bony hand holding her head down absolutely flat against the steel. She held still underneath her kickass great-grandmother as everyone else was screaming, crying, and wetting their pants.

After too long of a time spent kissing the bottom of a dirty milk truck, the shooting stopped. The weeping and sniffing went on for a while. A cloud of grey smoke wafted in through the holes, and Dakota began coughing. Liv lifted her head as Grandma let up on the pressure. She could see that the tank was a hell of a lot brighter now. Hundreds of bullet holes made the stainless-steel look like a macramé vest. The intense lights outside the tanker threw beams across the smoky interior like lasers.

All very pretty if you didn't consider that was an attempt to blow their heads off. They all sat there for a moment, just happy to have a pulse. Then, some old lady was talking to them over a PA system.

Liv couldn't hear every word, her ears were still ringing, but Grandma recognized the voice. She shot to her feet like she had been hit by cattle prod.

"You've got to be fuckin' kidding me!" was the first thing she said.

POST-APOCALYPSE MALAISE

The woman on the PA had said "No sudden moves," which was not as simple as Chris had thought when he was trying to wrench open the top hatch of milk truck that had just been shot up like a lace curtain. The hatch made a horrific screech as he pried it free of the deformed ring of steel around it. He stuck his head into the opening as soon as could push the insulated top out of the way.

"Everybody okay down there?" he called.

There was a sarcastic chuckle somewhere down below. He considered that a good sign.

"Could you come back in a couple minutes?" Liv replied. "We're getting our mani-pedis."

"Nobody shot? No broken bones?"

"Just some bumps and bruises," Olivia said. "We're damned lucky."

"Lucky and pissed," Grandma yelled. "Get me out of here right now!"

Chris reached both arms down to her as Olivia and the boys

boosted her up. She came up quickly, weighing no more than a hundred pounds dowsed in spoiled milk, and he deposited her on the open grid catwalk. Dakota came up next, standing on Olivia's shoulders. Then it was his Liv, and Cesar. All three kids looked a bit stunned from their night and the ride from the dairy.

Liv went to Grandma quickly and wrapped her arms around her waist. The older woman put a protective arm around Liv.

It must have been a very strange ride in that milk tank.

He and the boys all hunched down to rescue Olivia. He hung on to her a little longer than necessary, even though she smelled horrible. She felt good in his arms, and that was all that mattered in the world. At least for the three seconds before the woman on the PA spoke again.

"Everybody's out now. Please climb down from the truck and enter the compound through the outbuilding on the right."

Chris stepped away from Olivia, suddenly feeling guilty and embarrassed, though he didn't know why.

Grandma looked over the edge of the catwalk and spit. "Fuck you, you squirrel-loving cunt! We didn't come all this way to be eaten by your fucking tree-rats."

Chris was shocked. He said nothing, but his face must have given him away.

"Oh, grow up, Christopher. Sometimes, profanity is the only reasonable response." She jabbed a finger towards the ground. "And, look. We're still surrounded by those furry little bastards."

Chris looked down, and his stomach flipped over beneath his ribs. Dozens, perhaps hundreds, of rodents were below them. Every color and type of squirrel was represented, all slowly moving toward the silo. Many were covered in blood.

Olivia squealed at the sight and moved as if she were looking for someplace to run.

Chris took her wrist and held her in place. There was only eighteen inches of diamond grid metal below them, and then nothing but killer squirrels to either side.

The boys were making anxious noises, too, but Liv had the steely-eyed squirrel-hating glare that seemed to run in the female side of his family. Rafael and Vizcarra, who had been on the ground when he last looked, were standing on opposite running boards. Each had the look of a dangerous man calculating his odds against a thousand tiny enemies.

"My babies are no longer dangerous to you," the PA woman declared. "They are well-fed. They will be sleeping this meal off for days."

"Dangerous?" Grandma screamed. "Dangerous? Why don't you come up here, and I'll show you dangerous!"

"I would just as well like it if you came down to me, Iris." It was hard to tell at one-hundred and twenty decibels, but the amplified voice sounded smug to Chris, and just a little bit familiar.

"Officer Carnicero," the voice continued, "would you please help the crazy old squirrel lady down?"

Rafael, still bandaged from his last encounter, looked dubiously at the slow-moving river of fur and teeth beneath him.

"Don't worry, you're perfectly safe."

Rafael grimaced and set one foot down from the driver's side running board. With both feet on the ground, he stood stock still, holding his breath and waiting to be eaten.

The lethargic squirrels just trudged on toward their home. They adjusted their paths to avoid his ankles and then went on as if he weren't there.

Rafael shrugged and moved cautiously toward the ladder at the back of the truck. He looked like a man in a minefield. Still, he shuffled on steadily.

Just as he reached the rear tires of the trailer, one of the oversized Rottweiler squirrels bumped into him. It had somebody's hand in its mouth for a midnight snack, and it wasn't looking where it was going.

Rafael froze.

The killer rodent growled, slid between Rafael's legs, and went on its way.

Everyone started breathing again once he made it to the ladder. He held his arms up to Grandma as she descended in a sonic cloud of grunts and mumbled obscenities. She was in no better mood on the ground and surrounded by squirrels. Rafael silently warned her to behave. The woman on the PA put in her two cents worth. "Please don't kick my babies. They may not be hungry, but they will still protect themselves."

Grandma thrust her hands in her pockets and folded down on herself in a sullen funk.

Chris kept on the task of shepherding the kids down from the tanker.

The PA voice spoke again once they were all on the ground. "Would you all please take the door to the right?" she purred. "And, Corporal Carnicero, would you please leave your gun on the ground? It would only get you in trouble."

Rafael straightened up and glared at the PA speaker as if he were about to argue. Two of the sentry guns swiveled to bear down on him with a mechanical whirr that sounded like the approach of angry bees. Rafael frowned and placed the pistol at his feet, all the time handling it with only two fingers.

"And you, in the bloody white suit. Do you have any weapons?"

Vizcarra held open his jacket to reveal a sweat-stained silk shirt and an empty holster.

"Very good. The way in is over here."

A light suddenly illuminated the tiny concrete building beside the half-open silo door. The door unbolted with an audible buzz and a click.

Vizcarra gallantly gestured for Rafael to go first. He muttered something that started with *puto* and ended with *su madre*. He waved for the others to follow him as he headed for the entrance to the silo complex. As the others did, the sentry guns followed them like disapproving chaperones.

SQUIRREL CENTRAL

The lights blinked on as they moved farther into the underground tunnels and went out after they passed. This creeped out Liv more than hanging out in Cesar's House of Horrors, or watching Grandma's squirrel torture porn. The darkness that collapsed on them as they went deeper felt like it could be hiding anything: a masked maniac with a pickaxe, a kill-crazy mutant beast, maybe a flesh-melting blob of alien protoplasm. It could be almost anything, even an ass full of girl-eating squirrels.

Liv squeezed Grandma's hand and stuck close. The two of them were second in the parade down to Squirrel Central.

Cesar's angry uncle took the lead and kept the drug lord's jacket collar knotted up in his fist to make sure he didn't wander off too far.

Dad was right behind them, making noises like he was there to protect them, but Liv thought he wanted to stick close to the only person who frightened the squirrels.

A left turn brought them to the elevator lobby. A car waited for them with the doors open.

"Please, step inside," said the voice over the PA.

Liv had a natural impulse to protest, but the last time she said anything was met with a threat of flooding the complex with killer rodents. Dakota and Cesar nearly wet themselves then, so Liv chose to play nice.

The bunch of them fit easily into the shiny, metal box. It must have been the freight elevator. As it started to drop, she half expected cheesy Muzak to come through the speakers. "The Girl from Ipanema," maybe. All she heard was the sound of Grandma grinding her dentures in anger.

The car lurched and the lights flickered. Liv felt her stomach rise up to collide with her heart.

"Great," she muttered. "We survive the squirrels to be killed by the elevator."

Cesar and his uncle swiveled their heads around to glare at her.

"Sorry," she said as she shuffled closer to her father.

When the doors opened again, with them being what felt like maybe a mile underground, Liv saw a long dark passage. It was lined with cables and gigantic shock absorbers ending with a dimly lit room. Someone sat in a chair, but all the light was behind her, making it impossible to see her face. Liv had had a wild guess about the Sciuriologist's identity, but it was too crazy for her to say out loud.

"Please, come closer," the woman said in an amplified voice.

"You bet your sweet ass I will." Grandma barreled out of the elevator right at the woman in the chair. The rest of them did their best to keep up.

Liv hear a loud "thwap," and Grandma stopped suddenly. She

fell backwards on her ass, clutching her forehead where she'd hit it.

"Oh, and do be careful of the polycarbonate wall at the end, there." The voice sounded even smugger than before.

Dad and Cesar's uncle rushed over to lift her back to her feet and check her out. As they were doing that, the corporal put a hand on the small of her back and then froze for just a fraction of a second.

The two locked eyes, and he nodded minutely before he let her go. The whole silent exchange could only mean one thing: Grandma was packing.

The woman in the chair didn't seem to notice. This close, Liv could see she wore a white lab coat and black rubber gloves. She had one of those giant Indian killer squirrels cuddled up in her lap, and she stroked its fur steadily. It was still hard to see her face, but the stand-up bun of hair on the top of her head gave her a silhouette that was really hard to disguise.

"I do hope that didn't hurt too much."

"Let me in there," Grandma replied, "and I'll show you hurt, Janene."

The rest of the people on this side of clear wall got all worked up and noisy, except for Liv. She walked up to stand beside Grandma and put her hand on the clear plastic.

"Give it up, Ms. Brodnansky. The Bond Villain thing isn't working for you."

That shut everybody up on her side of the wall. Brodnansky chuckled, actually sounding a little like a super villain, and switched on the lights with a control pad on the arm of her chair.

"Clever girl." She stood and walked over to them, carrying that oversized rodent in her arms. "She must get it from you,

Iris," she said. "You were always the smartest, the prettiest, the most ambitious."

"I was just lucky," Grandma said. "When did you become the craziest?"

"Ooo, so hurtful." Brodnansky put down the animal, and it followed her as she paced back and forth in front of the wall. "Does she get that from you, too? The willingness to climb over anyone to get what you want? The utter disdain for other people's feelings?"

"You're the one that just killed hundreds of people, you psycho."

"All as a tribute to *you*." Brodnansky tilted her head as she looked Grandma over. "Oh, dear, you look like you been run through a car wash. Would you like to come in here and sit for a bit?"

She gestured toward the airlock door to the left, a revolving cylinder with offset doors. It swiveled around to invite Grandma inside.

"What would make me think that I would ever step out alive if I went in there?"

"That would be no fun," Brodnansky said. "There's so much more I'd like to show you."

She stood like a mannequin, her open hand beckoning towards the entrance, a creepy smile frozen on her face.

Grandma growled under her breath and headed for door.

Liv started to follow. So did Dad and Cesar's uncle.

"Just her!" Brodnansky shouted. The amplified voice felt like a slap across the back of the head.

Liv stopped where she was.

Of the bunch of them here in this bunker, Grandma seemed the best equipped to slap the living shit out of the other old lady.

The airlock cycled through, and Grandma stepped out the other side. She held her hands up and nodded to the multiple monitors on the wall behind them.

"So what is it you want to show me so badly? I've got all the squirrel documentaries I could ever want."

"Not these. This is brand new. Raw footage."

Brodnansky picked up a remote. The rodent at her feet chattered at Grandma angrily. She growled and muttered back.

Brodnansky flicked on one screen that Liv recognized as downtown Crickson. It showed an old woman in a cardigan and jeans being swarmed by a bunch of giant killer squirrels in front of the video store. She went down swinging as the squirrels tore at her and snarled like wolves.

"You remember Betty Lou Hellinger? She spread a rumor that I was caught *in flagrante delicto* with Javier Estevez under the bleachers our sophomore year. Made my life a living hell."

Another screen flicked on. A woman of about Grandma's age was tackled and smothered in a blanket of grey squirrels twice her weight.

"And Clellia Bedford, the one who pulled the fire alarm right after gym class our junior year. She thought it was very funny to see me wet and naked in the parking lot." Brodnansky smiled at Grandma. "She's not laughing now."

Three more screens lit up, all of them showing different angles of the same scene: the milk truck driving away from the dairy as it exploded. Liv had to admit that it was a hell of a lot scarier looking from the outside.

"Here, I have you, willingly blowing up your livelihood just to kill a few thousand squirrels. Positively delicious."

"Come with me to the Fernbridge branch, and we'll do it all over again. You can watch from inside."

"Not until you see everything, and everyone, you love die in the most horrible way I can imagine." The mad squirrel scientist flicked her eyes at Liv and her Dad and then bared her teeth.

Dad closed in and wrapped an arm around Liv's shoulder to pull her close. She patted his hand gently, but she wasn't scared, she was pissed. So was Grandma, it seemed.

"Jesus Fucking Christ, Janene! What the fuck did I ever do to you? We were best friends until you disappeared after graduation."

"You have no idea, do you?"

"If I had the slightest glimmer, I would admit to it before you feed one more innocent person to the squirrels!"

Brodnansky, shaking her head, walked up to the plastic barrier across from where Liv stood.

"Did you know that your great-grandmother was the Humboldt County Dairy Princess of Nineteen-fifty-five? With skin like cream and hair the color of butter, she was the most beautiful girl in the county."

"What?" Grandma snarled. "Were you jealous?"

Brodnansky winced in pain. "You could have had any boy you wanted. Why did you have to take Delbert Smithson? He and I were in love."

"Delbert?" Grandma got up in her face. "He and I were just friends, that's all."

"Then why did he take off with you on a six-month road trip that year?"

Grandma ground the heel of her palm into her forehead, a gesture she resorted to when faced with monumental idiocy. Like Dad's love life.

"Delbert," she explained slowly, but far from calmly, "came along to help with my makeup and clothes on the pageant circuit. There never was anything physical between the two of us."

"So you say." Brodnansky went back to pick up her killer squirrel and stroked it a little too energetically. Liv thought that she would always be gentle with something that could eat her face.

"Jesus H. Christ!" Grandma finally exploded. "When he left me, he went off to Vermont to open a bed and breakfast with my hair stylist. How much gayer can you get?"

"It must be something in the water," Dad quipped.

Liv glared up at him. Cesar's uncle, on the other side, caught him in a crossfire.

"You broke my heart, you clueless dairy queen!"

The brown and tan rodent squeaked in distress as she squeezed it in her arms.

Grandma circled away from Brodnansky, once again, with hand to head.

"You are delusional, you know that? You are absolutely out of your mind."

"Perhaps," Dad muttered, "this isn't the best time to go down that particular conversational path?"

"Yes, Ms. Brodnansky," Cpl. Carnicero said in his soothing cop voice. "Maybe, we could all sit down, lock up the squirrels, and talk this over."

As the adults tried to defuse the situation with Ms. Brodnansky, Liv felt a cold rage filling up her gut. Mom and Dad had done their stupid best to destroy her life and tear her away from everything she knew and loved. Crickson was redneck dairy purgatory, but at least it was the same every day, and she had a couple of friends to complain with. Then, the Squirrel Lady decided to get nuts, and everything was destroyed all over again.

"Wait a minute," Liv said. "Are you telling me that all this, the death and fire and explosions and the sheer terror of riding in a milk tanker as it is getting blown up, all of THIS, including almost getting KILLED, was over A BOY?" Liv was breathing a little heavy by then.

Everyone else was holding their breath.

Ms. Brodnansky put down her pet and strode over to another control panel.

"There is no "almost" about it, little girl. I always keep a few hungry squirrels in reserve, in case I have unexpected guests." Brodnansky hit a button, and there was an echoing metallic noise not too far away in the complex. "They'll be here any second."

MORE LATIN SPICE

C hris, being by nature and training an engineer, made a quick assessment of the situation: three exits from the space they were in; no loose items that could be used as tools, levers or weapons; no loose panels that could be pried free. He was still standing and thinking when he felt a tug on his collar back the way they came.

"For God's sake," Rafael shouted. "Run, *pendejo!*"

Chris took the first two or three steps leading with his neck as Rafael dragged him along. They collided with Cesar and Dakota coming their way.

"No, Tio Rafael, the other way! I heard the doors opening behind us."

"Are you sure?" Rafael asked as he released his grip on Chris. The two Carniceros wheeled around each other briefly as they decided which way they were running.

"We've gotten real good at this running from junk yard dogs," Cesar said.

Liv planted her feet. "Are you kidding? I was with you two the last time."

Chris grabbed Liv by the wrist and pulled her along. If they were all going to die down that direction, they would all die together. Heading back toward the wall of bullet-resistant polycarbonate, he was looking Ms. Brodnansky in the eye as she gloated.

That, or course, meant she wasn't watching Grandma pull out the two-foot section of copper pipe and valves she'd been clenching between her butt cheeks the entire time they'd been underground. With a shriek like an angry mountain lion, she swung overhead with both hands to catch Brodnansky between the shoulder blades. The two old women went down in a pile.

Chris kept running and dragging. He knew there was nothing he could do there.

The scientist cried out in pain as Grandma had one hand on the back of her neck and brandished the pipe with the other. Brodnansky called out what sounded like commands. That was about the time the giant killer squirrel got into the fracas.

Grandma was ready for it and swung at it like a furry piñata.

That was all he ever saw. They ran like scared little rabbits into the pitch-black tunnels until they could think of something better to do.

Rafael took the lead with the high-power flashlight from his belt and his holdout revolver from his ankle holster in his right hand. Six rounds of twenty-two ammunition was no match for a herd of animals that could gnaw a cow down to the bones, but it was all he had. As they pushed on down the passageway, he scanned the walls and floor for anything that could be turned into a weapon. The ceilings were packed with pipes of various sizes, and electrical conduits ran along one wall. Gigantic hydraulics held up the floor. Everything was bolted down and painted government institutional green and absolutely useless.

A jolt of pain ran up his right leg as he twisted his knee going around a corner. It was a reminder that he had made a two-point landing coming off the truck hood in the dairy: his knee and his forehead. Normally, that would have been on the top of his mind but, at the time, he was being eaten by squirrels. Pretty much every major part of his body had teeth marks in it, and it all stung like a bitch.

He looked over his shoulder, past the crowd of friends and family navigating by cell phone light. No visuals on the squirrels yet, but he thought he heard their chattering. The little bastards were probably going to eat them all if he didn't come up with something brilliant soon.

Ten more feet down the tunnel, and he found exactly what he needed. He was so thrilled that he shouted out loud before he even thought, *"Chinga su madre, ardillas!"*

He speed-limped over to the glass door and popped it open. His luck held so far, as there was still a canvas hose and brass nozzle in place.

"What did he say?" asked Liv.

Rafael blushed for a second at the thought of translating that to a twelve-year old girl, but Cesar stepped up. Holding his fingers apart to show *un poco*, he said, "It's basically "Yo momma, squirrels," with a bit more Latin spice."

Rafael uncoiled the fire hose onto the floor and checked for weak spots under the light. Without looking up, he told Cesar *Thank you* for the family-friendly translation. Then, he turned on the spigot. The hose straightened itself with only a half-dozen minor spurts along its length.

"So, Sheriff," said Chris, "we're going to be turning the fire-hoses on the protestors?"

"Something like that." Rafael picked up the nozzle and opened it up just a bit. The stream was good and strong. "A full pressure jet could knock a grown man on his ass. It should lift even the biggest of those furry bastards into orbit."

"Sounds like fun," Dakota said.

"No, it doesn't," Olivia replied. "Only horrible people enjoy torturing animals."

"And it's against the law besides," Rafael added. "So, all of you, find a way out of here. I got this."

"You can't stay behind!" Olivia said. "They'll eat you alive."

"That job's already half done. I'm beat to shit, and my right knee is about to lock up. If we have to run, I'd only slow you down."

"He's right, guys." Cesar's voice was shaky, but he spoke loud and clear, like a man. "The only way the fire hose will work is if he keeps spraying until the squirrels drown, or give up the fight."

He gave Rafael a quick hug. "See you on the topside, Tio Rafael."

Rafael nodded grimly. The others, except for Chris and Vizcarra, hugged him and stepped back quickly. Chris rocked on his feet from side to side, but finally came over.

"I'm going to have to buy you a beer after we all get out of this. We can talk. But, right now, I hear squirrels."

Rafael nodded again, not wanting to admit what he felt at the moment.

Chris pulled him into a bear hug and slapped him on the back, the way straight guys do to prove they're not gay. It hurt like hell.

"*Pendejo*," he said through the pain.

"Pencil-thin mustache," Chris replied.

He herded up the kids and pushed them down the passage way as fast as they could move by cell phone light.

Rafael braced himself against the wall near the spigot. He held the flashlight along the brass nozzle so he could see what he was spraying. Now, all he had to do was wait.

It was only a minute or two before the swarm of squirrels arrived. They filled the corridor floor from wall to wall. Some of the smaller ones ran along the equipment mounted on the walls.

Rafael switched on the spray and began hosing the rodents down. The wall runners flew backwards several feet and disappeared into the darkness with a squeal and a splash.

The swarm on the floor came at him like a single fluid mass like a mudslide with sharp teeth.

He'd hit the front line and push it back maybe two feet, but the squirrels behind them pushed back. Rafael played the hose across leading edge back and forth, an endless task like pushing back the ocean with a garden hoe. He just hoped the little bastards got tired of this before he did.

THE SHAFT

Olivia herded the children through the dark, as quiet and shaken as mice creeping along the floorboards of a cat shelter.

After several false starts, Cesar finally asked, "Do you think my uncle, and your Grandma, are really all right?"

She had been too caught up in the momentary goal of pushing them all up, and out, to think about who they left behind. She wrapped up Dakota and Cesar in a hug. "Don't worry. Your uncle is the toughest man in town. And, Grandma Day, she's even tougher."

Liv stood apart.

Even in the dark, Olivia could tell she was miserable.

Chris stood behind her, clearly feeling just as bad.

"I feel horrible leaving them behind," Liv moaned. "I feel like such a coward."

Olivia looked to Chris to step in but, he was, as usual, clueless.

Rafael's prisoner Vizcarra spoke up, instead. "I will tell you, as a long-lived individual with much experience, that there is no sin in running away from an opponent with superior firepower. Especially a horde of flesh-eating squirrels. They are intrinsically terrifying."

The boys chuckled at that.

Chris finally worked up the courage to speak, "Look. Liv, I know I'm the crappiest father in the world, but I just wanted to say—"

He was drowned out by a blare of feedback from the speakers above them. Then, a woman's voice came through, loud and clear. "Why won't you die, you squirrel-mongering BITCH!"

Crashes and animal squeals played through the PA.

Dakota giggled to himself. "I don't think *that's* what you meant to say!"

Olivia slapped him on the top of the head, not hard, just with enough force to remind him that he was being an adolescent and he should stop right now.

"Someone must have hit the *talk* button while they were trying to kill each other," Chris muttered.

"That's Grandma!" Liv practically lit up at the sound of her voice. "She's alive."

"Are you sure?" Chris muttered.

Another woman's voice screamed, "Chew her eyes out, Hieronymus!"

The transmission degenerated into a series of grunts, shrieks, and animal squeals, to be followed by several seconds of what sounded like someone striking a cabbage with a baseball bat.

Vizcarra nodded agreeably.

"I would say that *la abuela asesina* is doing just fine."

"Yeah, but this noise," Chris said, "is going to attract every squirrel in the place."

Cesar, the only one with a scientific brain amongst them,

aimed the light from his phone at the PA speakers and their cables.

"I'd say these speakers extend through the entire complex. The noise won't *lead* the squirrels to any one place..."

"Batter up," shouted Grandma. There was another crunchy thud heard over the PA and then squeals and crashes.

"You bitch!" shrieked the other old lady. "I'll kill you, myself!"

"But it could agitate every squirrel down here," Cesar concluded. "We may want to start running soon."

"Great plan," Chris said. "Let's go."

He and Olivia bundled up the kids and herded them down the passageway as two old women battled to the death in the control room. It was the strangest radio program she had ever heard.

The PA system cut out eventually. Chris couldn't say why, but what he heard in the silence afterwards disturbed him even more. The hiss of the firehose against concrete mixed with the squeals of hundreds of rodents. Rafael's inarticulate cries cut through it all at the end. Then, there were gunshots.

"That is a bad sign," Olivia whispered.

They needed no special urging to get the kids to run. It took just a couple of minutes to reach the end of the corridor. It was a curved wall, like the outside of a concrete cylinder.

The center was occupied by a pressure door large enough to accommodate a minivan. Chris recognized it right away. "This is the launch tube," he said. "The missile would have been housed here."

"We saw the squirrels crawling back in the top of this tube

when we came in," Vizcarra observed. "I don't think this a door we want to be opening."

"They're tired," Cesar replied, "and they've eaten. Those squirrels won't be interested in us."

The boy pointed down the tunnel, where the sounds of claws on metal and grinding teeth grew louder. "I'd say *those* squirrels *are*."

Vizcarra looked Chris in the eye, silently pleading for adult solidarity.

Chris shook his head. "We either go in there and risk a horrible death, or stay here and have one. Our choices are limited."

Chris turned to bring Olivia into the discussion.

She stood behind her son, arms draped over his shoulders, her eyes wide. For the moment, she didn't favor either choice.

"Let me take a look," Cesar volunteered. "We need to see how bad it is."

Chris already had his hand on the steel ring of the door lock. He spun it counterclockwise to undog the latches. "Like hell you will. You're just a kid."

Chris cut him off before he could make any argument. "We're going to pry this door open only enough for me to squeeze through. I'll go in, look around, and then come back. You all lean on the door, in case you need to close it real fast."

"Why would we do that?" Liv snapped.

"Well, if I'm writhing on the floor screaming, 'Please, kill me,' and I'm covered in squirrels," Chris shrugged, "then that would be a good reason."

"Not funny, Dad."

Chris felt the locking mechanism release. He pulled on the ring, and the door slowly opened.

"You never laugh at my jokes."

He put his arm through the crack between the hatch and jamb. Nothing inside gnawed it off. He put his weight against the huge chunk of steel, and it moved as if it weighed only twenty pounds. The U.S. Air Force always hired the best engineers.

"We need to get some intelligence." He could tell that Liv was petrified because she didn't respond to that straight line. Chris slipped through the gap and nearly lost his footing on the other side. The grid work of the platform was coated with a mix of squirrel shit, piss, and God knows what else. It smelled like a portable toilet at the end of a summer pierogi festival. He slid all the way through to look around.

The bottom of the launch tube was a toilet. Fecal matter covered everything and piled up along the walls. The metal platforms only extended a few feet, leaving an open pit in the center filled with fermenting squirrel guano. Bones and hair punctuated the unrelenting shit, remnants from hundreds of meals. Piles of ash still smoked on the platform, and they gave off the sickly-sweet smell of pot.

No wonder they hit town with the munchies.

Breathing through his mouth, he stepped close to the edge to look up the shaft. Faint, red work lights shone enough for him to see a vertical jungle of vines and leaves woven through the walkways, ladders and conduits. At the very top of the mass of dried vegetation and steel was the sliver of orange light visible through the gap of the concrete blast door. The gigantic nest was strangely quiet, as it seemed that every one of the surviving squirrels was sleeping off its meal of Crickson, CA.

Chris did some quick calculations in his head and came up with the stupidest idea he'd ever had since he invented his first squirrel launcher.

He crept back out into the corridor. As the others pushed

the door closed, he sucked in the relatively clean air of the tunnels.

"Well," he began, "I've got good news, good news, and bad news."

"Good news first, of course," said Vizcarra.

Chris held up his index finger. "Good news: I didn't get eaten. Ten points to House Carnicero for that."

Cesar beamed, and the boys high-fived each other.

Chris held up another finger. "Good news: I found a way out."

There wasn't as much celebrating now because everyone saw what was coming next.

"What's the bad news?" Liv asked in a strained and all-too practiced voice.

"We have to go through a hundred and fifty feet of squirrels to do it."

THAT BURNING SENSATION

The reasoned debate over Chris's plan lasted all of thirty seconds and was made up of most of the words you can't say in a Disney movie. He was both distressed and strangely proud at some of the combinations Liv created, but there was no time for family bonding. He finally stopped all conversation with a simple question. "Where do you want to die, kids?"

The kids' mouths went tight, and their eyes grew wide, especially Liv's. Dad never went so dark, but it had been a long day.

He regretted his remark as soon as he let it slip. Chris stroked his daughter's matted hair and nearly kissed her filthy forehead. Of course, he didn't. She was still covered with fermented fox pee and rancid cheese.

He nodded to Vizcarra, and the two of them wedged open the door again.

Olivia rushed the kids into the squirrel nursery.

Chris hoped he wasn't making a fatal error as he dogged down the hatch behind them.

Cesar, the curious one, was already standing near the edge of the central pit. He was plotting a course up to the top.

"Those maintenance ladders along the edges are going to be our only way up," he pointed out. "The platforms, themselves, seem to be filled up with something, nests, I guess."

"How many squirrels are up there, waiting to eat us?" Dakota asked.

"It would take a genius to calculate that." Liv slapped the back of Dakota's head. "But only a fucking idiot would do it."

"Right." Dakota rubbed his head and stepped out of her reach.

Chris joined the little group. He half thought to warn Liv about language and beating up her friends, but he figured to give her a pass for the night. Instead, he joined Cesar in plotting the best ascent.

The boy stood at the edge of the cesspit in the center. With one eye closed, he sighted down his index finger as he ran up each ladder and across the railings to the next. He quickly ran through several combinations and then pointed at a ladder on the far side of the tube.

"That route would be the quickest way up," he told Chris. He pointed out the way, a zig-zag path that covered half of the tube, but avoided the spots where vegetation hung far out over the railings to make things dangerous.

"That's the best plan I've heard all evening," Chris said. He waved Olivia and Vizcarra over to join them. "Come on, we're getting out of here."

He ran through a quick recap of the escape plan. Olivia was on board, but the stranger in the white suit grimaced up at the blast door and the crescent of evening sky it revealed.

"When we get up there," Vizcarra said, "what do we do about the automated guns?"

"One miracle at a time, please."

Vizcarra scoffed at that.

"We can only hope that Grandma beats Brodnansky to death before we get up there."

"That's not a plan. It is a suicide note."

Chris turned to Olivia for support, but the prim smile on her face showed she had less faith in his stratagem than she had in men. He faced Vizcarra instead. "If you have a better plan, I would just love to hear it."

"I will simply hang back and avoid whatever eats all of you first. It has worked just fine for me so far."

Chris was going to come up with some brilliant argument, but the boys took the initiative. Sprinting for the ladder, Cesar shouted, "Race ya!"

His paler, softer friend ran to catch up with him.

Liv summed up the situation with the adults in one heavy-lidded, jaundiced glare. She chose to run with the boys.

"Are you crazy?" Olivia called in a hushed squeal. "This is not a playground."

The kids ignored her and were already five feet up the ladder.

"Hey," Chris shrugged and followed, "we wanted to get them out of here as soon as possible."

Olivia stuttered out the beginning of a response, but she did it on the move.

Vizcarra smirked and hung back, as he had promised.

By the time Chris had started his ascent, the kids were already crossing along to the right on the outside of the railings. They hung onto the top rail tightly and moved carefully with the accumulated leaves and vines brushing their faces and obscuring their footing. He had no complaint with how they were climbing, except for the fact that the kids had to do it at all.

Chris reached the first level and stretched for a handhold

around a nest full of torpid squirrels. His breath caught in his throat as he saw them, but they were too stuffed to care. Only one large rodent that was licking blood from its fur even seemed to notice. Chris leaned way back to avoid touching any vine, or twig, that might disturb them. A muscle in his back pulled just a bit as he did.

If he lived to see the morning, he was going to be a twitching bundle of fears and injuries. He was really hoping for the agonies of the damned tomorrow.

* * *

The PA system kicked back in after they had climbed three ladders and made four lateral moves. It put them at just below the halfway point.

"Where the hell are they?" an old woman's voice called out through multiple speakers in the nest. The chattering of thousands of disturbed squirrels came as a response from the dead vegetation along the walls.

Chris held a fingertip to his lips and waved upwards toward the next ladder.

Liv nodded and pressed the boys forward, extending the ten-yard lead they had on the adults.

"They're not in any of the passageways. No signs of bodies," the voice continued, sounding like she was talking to herself.

Chris tried to push a little more speed out of his climbing, but he was just about ready to curl up for a nap under a family of flesh-eating rodents. Olivia and Vizcarra looked no better.

"What the fuck!" the voice shouted. "How did you get into the nursery?"

Chris was pretty sure that the voice was Brodnansky now.

That meant Grandma was down and out for the count, probably being eaten by Hieronymus, the killer squirrel.

Chris came to one of the surveillance cameras mounted beside a ladder. He grabbed it and pulled it to aim down at the cesspit at the bottom of the silo. He flashed his middle finger in front of the lens as he went by.

"Oh, no, you're not getting away from me that easily," Brodnansky chortled. The enormous blast door above the silo began to grind closed. The six-foot chunk of open sky disappeared inch by inch.

That got Chris moving.

"Climb faster!" Olivia screamed. "Get out of here any way you can."

Dakota hung for a second from the latest ladder and looked down.

Liv smacked him on the ass and he bolted upwards, not looking down.

Chris began his lateral move two sections to the right.

"I can stop her from closing that door!" Vizcarra shouted.

When Chris looked down, a view that included Olivia, Vizcarra, and about a hundred feet of silo, the man in the blood-spattered suit held up a silver and turquoise lighter.

"If I set fire to these dry leaves, the whole place will fill up with smoke. If the doors close, all of her precious animals will be smothered."

Chris instantly realized that, if the squirrel lady didn't close the door up top, they would all be in one of those tin can blast furnaces he used to light charcoal with newspaper. Chris was too exhausted to put that into words. His response instead was, "Stupid, fucking idea!"

Vizcarra chuckled. "We don't have the time for you to get any smarter ones."

He backtracked some on the level below and put his flame to a nest that hung out over the railings. Just as expected, the dry leaves caught like paper.

The squirrels inside the nest began to scream.

Chris hung from the ladder. He was too tired to climb anymore, and Olivia had yet to catch up with him. He could take a short breather to watch the maniac below get them all killed.

"Stop that," the voice on the PA. "You'll all die!"

Vizcarra inched along the railing a few feet to set another nest behind him on fire. This time, an angry squirrel popped out of the foliage to growl at him. He waved the flame of the lighter in its face, no doubt expecting the animal to back away. It was only pissed off.

The fat red rodent about the size of a housecat spun and sank its teeth into Vizcarra's wrist. He dropped the lighter, which fell the hundred feet or so into the cesspit. Whatever gasses the manure pit created, they caught fire in an instant. Chris felt the shockwave and the heat as it rushed up the silo.

Vizcarra held on for dear life with his free hand as he tried to pound the squirrel against the railing with the other.

The animal savaged his hand and wrist with no sign of letting go, either.

Two other squirrels defending their nest leaped into the battle and dug their claws into his face.

He let go then, and the lot of them plummeted into the pool of flames and shit at the bottom. They disappeared beneath the surface and never came back up.

Chris hung there, breathless and stunned. Vizcarra really had murdered them. Already, his face and hands were getting warm, and the smoke stung his lungs. He considered, for a moment, simply letting go and ending it all. Nothing but some vague idea about life and Liv countered the argument in his brain. Then, there was a wrenching pain in his left ear.

Olivia had caught up to him on the ladder and had her fingers latched onto his ear like a set of lockjaw pliers. She pressed her face close to his and snarled. "I don't care how tired and beat up you are, you are going to climb up and out of here if I have to drag you the whole way by your ear! Do you understand me?"

Chris tried to nod, but that only hurt more.

Olivia released him and forced him up the ladder ahead of her.

He climbed as fast as he could. He could already feel the flames below heating up his ass.

LOWERING THE BAR

C hris heard the first scream when he had only two more ladders to climb. He looked up, but Olivia was just above him and seemed fine.

Squirrels passed him to the right, or the left, all silent and fixed on escape. Some carried pink, blind babies in their teeth.

He couldn't see what else might be screaming, the thick waves of smoke rising up the silo made it hard to see more than a few feet. The fumes burned his eyes and lungs, and the heat felt like it would melt the soles of his sneakers.

Then, Chris heard a crash and a second scream. This scream was one of pain, the first had been pure homicidal rage. He realized he was hearing the PA system again, and which voice was which was cleared up instantly.

"Goddamn it, Iris!" the second voice shouted. "Why can't you stay dead?"

"Let me show you why, you bitch!"

The sounds for a little while were only the soundtrack of a knock-down drag-out fight between two octogenarians.

Chris picked his way across the outside of the railing that led to the last ladder. His head felt light from all the smoke. In school, he had been taught that if you were in a fire, you needed to get down as close to the floor as possible. That's where all the good air would be. But this was all backwards: the bottom of the silo was on fire and he had his head in the chimney sucking up all the smoke. He shook his head violently to clear it.

He was at the bottom of the last ladder, and he looked up. The opening of the silo door was less than three feet above him, and the gap kept getting smaller. For a moment, the grisly image of the blast door catching him around the neck ran through his mind. It would pop his head clean off, like a dandelion, and drop his twitching body into the lake of fire as it closed.

Chris had trouble moving for a second.

He forced himself up one rung. Then, he heard the gunshot. The sounds of fighting stopped immediately, and he made out the very final sound of a body dropping to the floor.

Chris looped his elbow through the rung above him and clamped his hand on that wrist to keep from falling.

Someone was dead in the control room.

If he didn't climb the last ten feet, there would be somebody dead in the silo. He put his foot on the next rung and pushed up. He was just a little bit closer to fresh air, a little bit closer to Liv. And, yeah, just a bit closer to hundreds of angry squirrels.

"Are you all right, Chris?"

At first, he thought it was Olivia, but she was climbing for her life, reaching for the edge of the blast door from the top of the ladder. It was somebody on the PA. A man's voice. On an incredibly bad day it might be Rafael's.

"Almost there," Chris wheezed.

"Keep climbing, *pendejo*. We're going to try something down here."

"Okay. You do that."

Chris climbed another rung. If he jumped, he could touch the underside of the blast door. If he jumped, he would fall to his death in a pool of flaming squirrel shit.

He wasn't going to jump.

With an explosive hissing sound, clouds of white smoke billowed out of the vegetation along the walls. At first, Chris thought that something new had caught fire, or a pope had been elected. Then he realized it was the fire suppression system.

He took a deep breath of something approximating air and lurched up another rung. He did another and then another. He didn't want to be down there when the launch tube filled with Halon.

"Keep climbing, man. This is going to suck up all the oxygen in the room in sixty seconds."

"You're almost there, Chris," Grandma said. "I'm so proud of you."

He may have hallucinated that last part, but he kept moving, nevertheless. Three or four more flopping movements, and he was at the top of the ladder reaching up for the sky.

An arm reached down and grasped his.

He pulled and wriggled through the closing gap at the top of the silo. If he had had that dessert with dinner tonight, he would have never fit. He rolled over onto his back to see the stars and the lights of the missile compound. He laid like that for a long time, coughing and gasping, like a carp on the beach.

Olivia's soot-blackened face came into view. She might have been crying, but it could have just been smoke in her eyes. He smiled up at her.

"You rescued me," he slurred. "Any chance of mouth to mouth restitution?"

She slapped him on the forehead, but gently. "Dream on, you're still breathing. Come back to me when you stop."

She leaned down and kissed him on the spot where she had hit him. She pulled away and worked her tongue around as if she was trying to get a bad taste out of her mouth. "Gack," she said. "You taste like charred ham."

Grandma's voice boomed out through the above ground speakers like the voice of God. "Don't anybody move!"

Chris felt himself moving in spite of himself, being on top of the blast door as it closed the last few inches. A plume of white Halon vapor flowed out of the gap along with several dozen gasping squirrels.

"Where the fuck do you think we're going?" Liv shouted.

Of course, when he heard her voice, Chris popped up on one elbow to find her. Though it wasn't much, it was still technically moving. He quickly spotted Liv, Dakota, and Cesar standing on top of the dairy tanker. There were a few hundred pissed-off meat-eating squirrels between the kids and Chris. As he craned his neck around, he saw that there was a few hundred pissed-off meat-eating squirrels between him and everything else.

And half of them were glaring at him and Olivia. The silo door came to a loud and final stop. The noise was like a cement vault sliding in place over a coffin.

"Fffffuck," Chris said.

"Yeah, that," Olivia agreed.

"Don't worry," Grandma said. "We're working on something."

"Are you out of you mind?" Rafael said. "We're just as likely to kill them as the squirrels."

"The directions are right here. That bitch was always obsessive-compulsive about documentation."

"No, Iris."

"Look at camera three. They are all thirty seconds away from being squirrel chow."

Rafael sighed. It sounded like a wind storm over the PA system. "Okay," he said. "so we change all these settings then. Maximum size fifty kilograms?"

"Liv is kind of skinny. Let's make it thirty-five to be safe."

"Okay. And minimum size is reduced to zero."

Chris had no idea what was going on, but it was scaring the piss out of him.

"All right," said Rafael with a tone of finality. "Nobody move at all. We will be firing the sentry guns in three seconds."

"WHAT?" everybody above ground screamed.

"In three, two, one..."

Before anyone could say anything else, the automated guns let loose with the sound of a million angry bees. They swiveled back and forth, spitting fire and lead in deliberate arcs across the ground. Each shot hit a squirrel, and each hit reduced the animal to twitching limbs and a fine cloud of meat and fur.

Chris and Olivia threw themselves flat on the concrete blast door and covered their heads with their hands. He had no idea what actually happened for the next sixty seconds, but he swore he could feel the bullets fly over his back and graze his knuckles. Then the guns stopped.

He peeked out from under his hands and saw a landscape of liquefied squirrels and cordite smoke. On top of the tanker, the kids looked intact, each curled up in a fetal ball. Shaky and, perhaps, incontinent, but intact.

"ARE YOU DONE YET?" Chris screamed.

"Just one second," Grandma replied.

One of the guns fired a single burst. A nearby tree exploded into matchsticks.

"Sorry," Grandma said, "squirrels in the trees."

"So that's it?" he shouted. "It's all over? No more killer squirrels?"

"Yep," said Grandma with a satisfied chuckle. "Like the lady on the radio says, 'Karma is like a squirrel in a blender. What goes around comes around, and it's usually not very pretty.' "

"Great," said Olivia, "let's go home, then."

"Not so fast," Rafael said. He sounded nowhere near as happy as Grandma. "You all need to come back down here and see something."

SQUIRREL APOCALYPSE

None of the kids wanted to get back in the elevator. Liv was convinced there were still mutant killer squirrels wandering the underground compound. Cesar was justifiably concerned over the elevator and the fire in the launch tube. Dakota was scared by everything, including the possibility of giant spiders in the elevator shaft. Considering what they'd faced already, Chris didn't think that was a totally unreasonable fear.

Liv huddled against him on the way down, hanging on for comfort in a way she hadn't done in years. Olivia wrapped both of the boys up in her arms.

Yeah, I see decades of therapy for everyone in this box, Chris thought.

It took a minute or so, but the elevator doors finally opened on the same corridor which led to the control room.

Grandma stood just inside the clear plastic wall. Her clothes were torn and bloodied. Her face and hands were covered with deep scratches. The corpse of Hieronymus, the giant killer squirrel, was draped over the command chair behind her. On his back with mouth agape and one paw across his chest, he looked like the product of a Shakespearean death scene.

Her voice rang out across the PA system as they approached. "So. Do you see why I hate squirrels so much now?"

"Yes, but you're still crazy."

She pointed to the rotating cylinder airlock at the far end of the transparent wall. "Finally figured out how to wedge that thing open. Come on through."

With the invitation, Liv rushed over to Grandma and enveloped her in a flying hug.

The old woman was only partially unbalanced from the impact, but she groaned with pain as the girl squeezed her tight.

Liv stepped back quickly with a devastated look on her face. "I'm so sorry," she squealed. "I'm just so glad to see you alive."

"It's all right."

"You look like you were torn to pieces."

Grandma chuckled. "You should see the other ornery old broad in the fight."

With a nod, she indicated what looked to be a pile of dirty laundry in the corner. Ms. Brodnansky's clunky black orthopedic shoes stuck out from one end. The other end was covered in a spare lab coat which was slowly soaking up blood from what Chris guessed had been her head.

"Did you..." Liv pointed limply at the corpse. Her expression was distressed, proud, and frightened all at once.

"Nawww," Grandma said. "That was the heroic Corporal Rafael Carnicero, who came to the rescue of a defenseless old lady, at the last moment, with his very last bullet."

Rafael smirked at the characterizations, but said nothing.

Grandma leaned in conspiratorially and continued in a stage whisper, "Just between you and me, if I had done the deed, there'd be a HELL of a lot more blood spatter in this room. You know what I mean?"

"Grandma!" Liv exclaimed with a grin. "You are a homicidal maniac."

"Only when I need to be."

Cesar had been hanging back, looking as afraid of, as fearful for his uncle. "Not that I'm not happy, Tio Rafael" the boy said, "but how are you not dead?"

Rafael flashed a guilty grimace at Grandma.

Grandma flinched and then shrugged, silently urging him to say whatever awful thing they shared.

"Well, I was incredibly lucky," he said. "There's no way we could have really foreseen it." Rafael stopped there, looking too uncomfortable to go on.

Grandma picked up the thread of the story. "I had knocked out that dried up old cunt for maybe a minute..."

"Language in front of the kids," Chris said out of pure reflex.

"Fuck language. These kids saw people eaten alive by squirrels tonight. I don't think a little anatomy is going to traumatize them any more." She took a breath and went back to her story. "While the... *old bat*... was out, I started pressing buttons, hoping I could do something useful."

"She accidentally hit the door locks," Rafael added. "I heard the lock buzz just behind me as I was considering whether I would use my last bullet on myself, or try to outrun the few bastards I hadn't drowned."

"You were going to shoot yourself?" Olivia asked, clearly horrified.

"I wasn't going to be eaten by squirrels twice in one night."

"Wait a minute," said Cesar. "So you got out of the passage-ways just in the nick of time?"

"He was damn lucky," Grandma said.

"And, if we had stuck with you, we would have never had to climb up a vertical tunnel filled with killer squirrels?"

"Well.... No." Rafael tried a grin, but it failed horribly.

There was a three count of icy silence. Chris thought heard steam whistling out of a pressure container. Then, Olivia exploded:

"Rafael, you jack-booted, half-witted son of a fucking bitch!"

"It wasn't on purpose," Rafael said.

"I don't fucking care! You don't think some could have said something over the PA system?"

"Well, Brodnansky started killing me again right after that," Grandma muttered.

"Good! You deserve it! Do you know how many ways our kids could have died? The squirrels. The burning guano. Just the drop." Olivia stopped for a moment, her eyes wide. "Vizcarra, he did die because he climbed up the silo with us."

"Actually," Dakota said, "he died because he set the squirrels on fire, and that pissed them off."

"And he was actually a very bad man," Rafael said.

"That's not important." She held up her hands before her, as if she were holding up a concept too large for her son to grasp. "You could have died. And it would have been my fault, because I was doing what I thought was best, and I was wrong. I would have died a hundred times rather than let anything happen to you."

"That's true for any of us," Rafael said. He pulled Cesar into a hug, but gently, as if he might break, or break away.

Olivia wrapped her son up in a smothering embrace with a mumured promise that she might never let him go.

As Liv drifted over to Chris, Olivia pulled Rafael and Cesar into her orbit.

Eventually, they were all wrapped up in a huge dysfunctional family hug, except for Grandma, who had broken out the first-aid kit. She was daubing mercurochrome on her scratches and was in danger of painting herself completely orange.

"Didn't you have something for my grandson to look at?" She waved vaguely at the readouts on the wall. "By the way, we're still on fire over there."

Rafael broke free and headed over to a computer station on the far side of the control room.

Chris followed, starting to feel a bit deflated now that the adrenaline and terror had begun to wear off.

Rafael chuckled as he looked over his sooty and battered friend. "You look like you were hung up and smoked, like a *barbacoa*."

"Well, I sorta was." Chris ran a hand through his hair, which practically crackled from the grit and grime. "You, on the other hand..."

Rafael turned and grinned at him. Dozens of new pink adhesive bandages from the first-aid kit covered squirrel bites on his face, neck and hands.

"What do you think I look like?"

"You look like you were eaten by squirrels and shat out in multiple pieces."

"Well, I sorta was..." Rafael laughed, something Chris had never really seen, and then pulled Chris into a bear hug. He even slapped Chris three times on the back, hard enough probably to leave handprints under the shirt.

Chris just held on, grateful to have his friend back alive. When they broke the clinch, he still held onto Rafael's shoulders and looked him in the eye.

"Are we good?"

"Good?" Rafael rolled his eyes upwards in thought. "We're alive. Let's shoot for good next week."

"Good." Chris gave him a "thumbs up" and sat down in front of the computer. "So what the hell am I looking at?"

"Did you ever wonder how a retired government employee could buy a decommissioned missile silo and engineer a new species on her pension?"

"So we're looking at a conspiracy with deep pockets. And a twisted worldview." Chris began pecking away at the file system, and it led down a rabbit hole. Decades of back and forth communications. Emails and spreadsheets showed millions, if not billions, of dollars coming from someone called Ratufa. Whoever that was, Ratufa coordinated plans, genetic code, timing for attacks. As Chris dug deeper, he realized that this was the first evidence of an organization as big as ISIS, but dedicated to weaponized squirrels instead of religious zealotry.

"We need to get this to Homeland Security right away," Chris muttered.

"Can you upload this, or download it, or something?"

Chris frowned up at the deputy. "Sorry. I didn't bring along my hundred terabyte hard drive last night when I left the house."

"Smart ass." Rafael pointed at an icon on the screen labelled *Live Feed*. "What the hell is that?"

"Let's see," Chris said as he clicked it.

Large TV screens came to life all around the control room. They displayed outdoor closed-circuit camera video of different locations around the world.

Chris noted a few of the screens labelled: *Machida Risu-en, Tokyo; Parcul Central, Romania*; and *Olney, Illinois*. As the images changed on the screens, they all looked the same. Everywhere was destruction, fire, and debris. One camera showed people running and screaming. Another showed people being devoured.

All of his family and friends stared up at the multiple disasters and relived the horrors of the previous night because, absolutely everywhere, there were squirrels.

ACKNOWLEDGMENTS

No author really works by himself. I appreciate the contributions my son Aidan, my wife Kit, and all my friends and coworkers made, both in commission and omission. Thank you for your support.

ABOUT THE AUTHOR

Josef Matulich is an author, make-up artist, and retired mime who lives in a suburb of Columbus, Ohio. His previous occupations have given him a care-free familiarity with cows, explosives, mass spectrometers, and helium balloons which find their way into his fiction. When not involved in his corporate day-job, or creating funny/scary stuff, he assists his wife Kit in their semi-haunted vintage and costume shop.

He has never launched a squirrel in his life.

Made in the USA
Lexington, KY
29 November 2019

57772483R00146